TANNER'S LAST CHANCE

Ranz Tanner is down to six cents and a lame
horse when he defends a young Mexican
girl in a cantina fight; he shoots a man and
is sentenced to five years in Yuma Prison.
His pals should have named him Bad Luck
Tanner – every chance that comes his way,
he just naturally seems to pick the wrong
side. He can't even get to jail uneventfully.
When the man driving the prison wagon
kills Smocker MacDermit, the only son of the
wealthiest man in Adobe Falls, it triggers a
bloody range war and Ranz is right in the
middle.

TANNER'S LAST CHANCE

TANNER'S LAST CHANCE

by

Terrell L. Bowers

The Golden West Large Print Books
Long Preston, North Yorkshire,
BD23 4ND, England.

British Library Cataloguing in Publication Data.

Bowers, Terrell L.
    Tanner's last chance.

    A catalogue record of this book is
    available from the British Library

    ISBN   978-1-84262-916-1 pbk

First published 1991 by Avalon Books, New York

Copyright © 1991 by Terrell L. Bowers

Cover illustration © Michael Thomas

Published in Large Print 2012 by arrangement with
Golden West Literary Agency

The Golden West Large Print is an imprint of Library Magna
Books Ltd.

Printed and bound in Great Britain by
T.J. (International) Ltd., Cornwall, PL28 8RW

Chapter One

It was a filthy place to raise kids. A *niña* crawled about and played with the spittoon while her mother tried to attend to the dozen or so customers in the saloon.

Ranz Tanner sat in a corner of the room, sipping the beer he'd been nursing for over an hour. He was down to six cents and a lame horse. Broke and out of a job – that was about the usual status for him.

Instead of Ranz, his folks should have named him Bad Luck Tanner. He could not recall doing one thing right in his entire life. Every choice that came his way, he just naturally seemed to pick the wrong side or direction.

One of the Mexican kids ran through the place, chased by a second. Ranz figured that there were at least six of the little waifs. They scurried here and there. It reminded him of the rats in a Mexican prison, darting about, trying not to get stepped on, snatching food scraps from the prisoners. It appeared that water was scarce in that part of Arizona, because there was not a clean face among the kids.

He reconsidered that thought, for the eldest of the girls was serving the tables. She was probably in her middle teens and had gotten to the point in life where she cared about her appearance. She wore ragged clothes, but they were clean, and her shoulder-length hair was neat and brushed to a healthy sheen.

'Pardon, señor,' she said to Ranz in broken English. 'Want one beer more?'

'Thanks, but this will do me fine. I've got to get going.'

She probably did not understand very much of what he said, but she got the idea. She showed her teeth in a short, professional smile.

'*Gracias,* señor. Come again maybe.'

He should have emptied the bottle of its warm contents and walked out of the tavern. He had no reason to hang around. There was a job somewhere that would at least give him room and board for a day or two. All he had to do was find it.

'Hey, Bud! Give a gander at the little Mexican filly.'

Ranz eyed the three men at the next table. They wore the riding chaps of Texas drovers

– heavy, thick, shotgun-style leather chaps for bucking thorny brush. Ranz had been below the Pecos a few times and was familiar with the thickets and thorns that could peel a man's hide. He had worn out more than one pair of similar chaps.

Another of the trio leered at the young girl and spoke up. 'By gum, Cully, she be a fine-looking Mex.'

'Too bad she's only the age she is, Cully,' the third man spoke up from the table. 'Bet she'll be a real looker in a couple more seasons.'

The man called Cully reached out and grabbed the girl around the waist. She cried out in surprise as he pulled her down on his lap. It brought a round of laughter from the other two men.

'What do you say, little señorita? Want to dance and party with some nice Texas boys?'

She cried out something in Spanish. It was too fast for Ranz to pick up, but he knew she was frightened. He set his teeth and tried to keep his nose out of trouble.

'Please, mister!' the older woman called to them. 'Please let her go. I cannot do the work without her to help.'

'Maybe for a kiss,' Cully said, and he laughed.

11

Ranz sized up the three men. Cully was the big-mouth type, the guy who knew it all. He had an arrogant look about him and liked being the center of attention. The other two were cowboys, simple hands on a trail drive. They were looking for a little fun and diversion from the daily drudgery of hazing cattle and eating their dust.

The girl squirmed in Cully's grasp, but he held her tight. When she raked the side of his face with her nails, his fun came to a sudden end.

He let out a howl of pain and rose to his feet quickly. The action dumped the girl onto the dirt floor. Before she could scramble away, he caught hold of her hair and yanked her around. He slapped her cheek hard, and then pulled back his hand for a second swat.

'I wouldn't do that!' was all Ranz said, but it brought a sudden hush to the tavern crowd.

Cully glowered at him. 'See what she did to my face?' He pointed at the scratch marks, two of which showed blood.

'I'd say you asked for it, friend. She scratched you and you smacked her a good one. That ought to make it even.'

'Not by a long shot,' Cully said, glaring hard at Ranz. 'Who do these Mexicans think they are up here in Arizona Territory? Down Texas way, we know how to handle them.'

'I've seen your treatment of them on occasion,' Ranz replied with bitterness. 'This ain't Texas.'

Cully let go of the girl's hair. She crawled on all fours to get across the room, and cowered behind her mother. Cully did not give her a second glance. His attention was on Ranz.

'Better give me your name, saddle tramp, so's we can put it on your marker.' As he spoke, Cully kicked his chair out of the way. His hand dropped over his gun, removing the leather thong with his thumb.

Ranz thought that the other two might join up against him, but they were willing to leave it to Cully, who was able-looking and probably formidable in a fight.

'I'm not looking for trouble, fella,' Ranz told him quietly. 'Don't push me into something you'll not live to regret.'

Cully laughed in contempt. 'Hear that, boys? I'm not going to live to regret killing this saddle tramp.'

Ranz did not have to remove the safety thong from his own gun. He made a habit of never securing the gun when he entered a town or encountered other men on the trail.

More than once it had saved his hide.

Cully licked his lips, his eyes alive with anticipation. Ranz had seen that look before. There would be no talking to the man. He had made up his mind. He would draw and fire. It would be either him or Ranz, and perhaps both of them would die.

'Dang it all, Cully,' one of his friends said quietly, 'you don't got nothing to prove by killing some saddle bum. There might be a lawman about.'

Cully's grin turned into a sneer. 'I aim to rid the country of a dirt-bag, boys. You sit tight and watch me take him.'

He was quick. His hand was a blur, snaking down and snatching his gun from its holster. He brought it up with a practiced draw, aligning the sights, his finger tightening on the trigger.

But Ranz's gun belched fire and lead, two rapid blasts that spelled an instant death for the cowboy.

Cully backed up a step from the impact of the two slugs. His lifeless finger could not pull the trigger on his own gun. Glassy-eyed, he swayed for a second, then fell flat onto his face.

'I find the defendant guilty of first-degree

manslaughter,' the judge pronounced sentence. 'And I hereby sentence you to five years in the Yuma Territorial Prison.'

The announcement brought a round of catcalls and jeers, but that was all.

'Approach the bench, Ranz Tanner.'

Ranz walked forward, the chains on his wrists and legs rattling from the motion. He stopped in front of the judge and bore into him with burning eyes. 'That other fella drew down on me. I had no choice, and you darned well know it!'

The judge nodded toward the crowded barroom. 'Think straight, Tanner. The place is full of cowboys and friends of the man you killed. If I declared you to be innocent, we'd both be strung up. You may not think so, but I'm saving your life.'

'Five years in Yuma is a funny way of saving a man's life, Judge. A good many men die there every year.'

The judge leaned over, speaking so that only Ranz could hear him. 'I'll send off a letter once the cowboys see you hauled away in the prison wagon. I'll explain the situation to the warden and send along your pardon. You won't have to serve any time.'

Ranz studied the man. He had no reason to lie. If he so desired, he could have changed

15

his verdict and gotten him hanged on the spot. 'Are you on the level about this?' he asked the judge.

'I give you my word. By the time you get to Yuma, I'll see that you are a free man.' The judge looked around at the room full of cowboys. 'I think you'll agree that these fellows would not accept a verdict of self-defense. You would end up dead, and maybe me too, son.'

Ranz knew that the man spoke the truth. There were over thirty drovers from two different cattle herds in the room. The judge was saving his bacon the only way he could, and he would have to go through the motions of being taken to Yuma and then bide his time.

'Guess I've no choice but to do as you say, Your Honor.'

The judge looked around the room and banged his gavel on the desk. 'This case is closed,' he announced. 'Bar's open and the first round is on me!'

Ranz was escorted out by two armed guards. He would have to sit in jail until the prison wagon came through town. During the long trip to Yuma, he'd be hoping all the while that the judge would not forget his promise.

Chapter Two

The town of Adobe Wells turned out in full force to see the arrival of the prison wagon. Once a month it rolled through on its way to Yuma Territorial Prison. The arrival of the wagon stirred about as much excitement as the monthly stage run that brought mail and an occasional passenger.

Ranz slumped against the corner rails of the iron cage. He had his hat tipped low to shade his eyes and also to help keep the dust out of his face. After three days in the cage, he was covered with alkali dust and worn down like a pair of pilgrim's walking shoes.

From beneath the rim of his sweat-stained Stetson, his eyes swept over the throng of people. There were no more than twenty men, half that many women, and about two dozen kids. Because it was Sunday, everyone in the farming community was in town.

'He looks like a tough hombre,' one man said over the buzz of the crowd. 'What'd he do, Deputy?'

After spitting a stream of tobacco juice into the dust, Joe Brady puffed himself up like the braggart he was. From the way he talked, anyone would think that he had rounded up every bandit or killer in all of Arizona by himself.

'Caught him near Yellow Rock. He ran his horse aground and stood to make a fight. Killed three good men before he run out of ammunition. He'll hang high once we get him to Yuma.'

Ranz grunted. That showed how much people would swallow. No one wasted a prison wagon on a man who was heading for a noose. The nearest tree or a hasty rope over the livery hoist usually did the job.

Of course, the story was a fairy tale too. Joe had looked over the papers and read the five-year sentence. That was all he knew about the trial. But for Ranz to speak up against his word would only make traveling with him worse. No need getting on his bad side, what with two days of travel left.

When a young boy came a little too close to the wagon, Joe stuck out a warning hand, holding the whip he used on the six-mule team.

'Don't go no closer, boy. That there jasper might latch on to you and force us to let him out. I ain't letting no one become a hostage or any prisoner escape from me.'

A woman's hand shot out and caught hold of the boy's shirt. She just about yanked him off of his feet, pulling him away so quickly.

'Only one prisoner, Deputy?' a stern-looking woman asked.

Joe stretched and arched his back. 'Slow this trip. I got two more waiting down the road. Could be that we're cleaning up the Territory.'

'If you put Cochise and Geronimo away, then we'd all sleep better.'

'That ain't my job. We got the soldiers to do them chores.'

'Spending the night, Joe?' an elderly gent queried.

Joe nodded and jerked a thumb at the rear wheel. 'Maybe an extra day, Gus. That rim has separated, and I had to bind it together three times with wire. Reckon the local blacksmith can fix it.'

'What about your prisoner?' Gus asked.

'Stick him in your smokehouse, same as always.'

'For two days? In this heat?' Gus shook his white-capped head. 'That ain't rightly human.'

Joe laughed. 'Do him good. Might get him

19

ready for the likes of Yuma.'

'Thought he was going to hang,' someone remembered.

'Not until he's tried for them three men he killed during his capture. That might take a few weeks.'

The rear door swung open and Joe pulled out his pistol. He cocked it and held it pointed toward Ranz. It was part of the show. Everyone backed away to give Joe room to work.

Ranz wondered how he could have looked like much of a menace. He had shackles around his ankles and wrists, and a chain running between them. If he had tried to escape, he would have had to leapfrog his way across the open desert. He certainly couldn't have walked or run.

'Come on out, Tanner. And do it slow and easy. I'd hate to cheat the hangman.'

'You're a thoughtful man,' Ranz said. 'Here I was just thinking how you never thought of anyone but yourself. Makes me downright ashamed of myself.'

'Move it!' Joe growled.

Ranz was stiff and bruised from being bounced about in the back of the cage. He could not stand up, for the roof was only five feet from the floor. With the chains all rattling and dragging, he crouched down and made his way to the back gate.

'Get on down here,' Joe ordered, standing ten feet back from him.

'Give me a minute. I ain't used to packing so much jewelry around. Being such a kind-hearted soul, you wouldn't want me to fall and hurt myself.'

'You've a sassy mouth, Tanner. Could be that they won't find your humor very funny in Yuma.'

Ranz sat down at the edge of the wagon and got his feet on the ground. Then he stopped, as if thinking hard. 'The more you tell me about Yuma, the less I like it, Joe. Maybe I'll change my mind and not go.'

The deputy grew red in the face. 'You ain't got no choice! I'll blow your gizzard to bits if you try anything funny.'

'Don't worry about that, Joe. I doubt that I could do anything funny with you around. Seems that you steal the show at every stop with your tall tales.'

That brought a round of snickers and a few chuckles. It also put a dark frown on Joe's sunburned face.

'Walk ahead of me, Tanner. You get cute and I'll back-shoot you.'

Ranz tried to stretch, but the chains kept

him from lifting his arms. As he started off in the direction Joe indicated, the tightness in his muscles made him walk stiff-legged. The chains rattled and clanked all the way to the smokehouse.

The singular structure was made out of sod and clay bricks. The roof was of wooden slabs that had been covered with dirt. A few hardy weeds grew along the upper edge, which was a low place that collected moisture during a rain. A brick chimney protruded near the back.

Ranz stepped into the dark shed, which reeked of smoke from jerky and ham. Immediately his dry mouth began to water.

'Maybe I could trouble you for a little water, Joe. I wouldn't want to waste away during the night.'

'You'll get a cup with your meal, same as always.'

Ranz turned slowly and regarded the deputy with a sullen gaze. Unshaven, barrel-chested, with a thick neck and meaty arms, Joe was built like a bullet. Even so, Ranz wondered what it would be like to smash his ugly puss with a set of rock-hard knuckles. Somehow, he knew he would greatly enjoy that.

'Looks like I get my purgatory now. I expect that you'll get yours when you cash in your last chip.'

'Inside, Tanner. I've had enough of your mouth.'

Ranz took a step into the darkened room and the door slammed behind him. It took some time to adjust his eyes to the dark interior. There were no contents other than a stove and a number of hooks dangling from the ceiling. It took only one slow walk around to discover that there was no way out. Considering the shackles and chains, he could not have expected to escape from an open corral.

'What do you say, Ranz?' he asked himself aloud. 'Think this is any worse than your last hotel?'

He went to a corner and sat down on the ground. At least this floor didn't bounce and jar him around. It was stifling, muggy, and over a hundred degrees, but at least the room stayed in one place.

'Could be worse,' he answered himself after a time. 'They might have stuck me in here with bad companions. At least I don't have to keep an eye on my timepiece.'

Even as he spoke, he saw a dark shadow move along the ground. He swung a boot around and squashed the scorpion under his heel.

'Spoke too soon,' he said. 'I've got a few bad companions in here after all.'

Chapter Three

Duke MacDermit hammered the dinner table with his clenched fist. His eyes bore into his son, Stocker.

'You don't have to ride into Adobe Wells every blasted night, son. I should have never let them squatters take root. They steal my land, poach my cattle, and now they've got my son panting after some skirt. I rue the day I let the first settler squat on my land.'

Stocker laughed. He never took the old man too seriously. Duke rode the Cross M Ranch with razor-sharp rowels on his spurs and an iron hand. No one stood up to the range baron and lived to brag about it.

But Stocker was the man's only offspring. His younger brother had died by an Indian arrow, and his sister had come down with chicken pox during a visit with their uncle. Her death had left him the only immediate heir to the Cross M.

'Have you taken a good look at the Ankers girl lately, Pa? She's as pretty as a newborn heifer and sweet as sugar candy. I've a mind to marry her.'

'Why don't you do it then?' Duke advised. 'I'm tired of you always being gone. You ride into that shantytown to drink and gamble all night, chase women, and get into fights. You only come home to sober up and mend your aches and pains. A woman at the ranch might at least keep you here occasionally.'

'Cora is like a wild mustang, Pa. I've got to put a halter on her, then break her to rein. At the moment she thinks of herself as wild stock, free to roam where she pleases.'

'Ain't no nester woman going to turn you down, son. You're the catch of the entire Territory.'

Stocker stood up, his chest expanded in the same manner as his father. He showed a wide grin.

'I'll be back late, Pa. Send Locker out in my place tomorrow. He can ride herd on the boys until Keats shows up.'

Duke's head moved from side to side in a slow, negative motion. 'I went wrong with your rearing, boy. I let you mix with trash.'

Stocker chuckled. 'I'm headstrong and wild like you, Pa. You can't get used to looking in the mirror.'

Duke had to smile. 'You could be right.'

Stocker went out into the evening dusk.

He already had a horse waiting. That was Con Velarde's doing. The young gun was eager to get ahead on the ranch, and he was good company.

'You riding with me tonight, Con?'

The man smiled. As far back as Stocker could recall, Con never laughed. He smiled a good deal of the time, but he wasn't a cheerful sort. When his lips curled, it was about the same as a snake setting up to strike. Just because it wagged its tail or stuck out its tongue, that didn't mean it was friendly.

'You get to sleep late, Stocker. Your pa expects me to ride with the others at daylight. I'll stick here tonight.'

'Are you saying that I'm spoiled or something, Con?'

That same smile appeared. 'Or something, Stocker. You have fun.'

Stocker mounted and turned toward town. He was eager to set eyes on Cora Ankers again. She put a match to his blood and heated it to a boil. She was something he had to possess. It didn't matter that she shunned him and repelled his advances. He knew that she would come around. Who else was there in Adobe Wells?

It was past dark when the door was pushed

open to the smokehouse. Ranz had to blink against the bright glow from the lamp. He raised his hand to shield his eyes, and the motion rattled the chains.

A woman held the lamp high and then stepped into the room and looked at him. She appeared fairly youthful, but her brown eyes showed a degree of experience.

'Your keeper forgot all about you. I didn't wish to see you go hungry all night.'

His eyes adjusted to the light and he lowered his hand. With a sweeping glance, he appraised the woman. She wore a dress that had seen its best days. Her hair was under a bonnet and held in place by a yellow ribbon. Her bodice was a dull, button-up affair without any lace. Dressed in such a manner, she appeared rather plain. She had a plate in one hand and a cup tucked under that same arm.

'If you'll remain where you are, I'll give you food and water. I have the only boarding-house in town. It's part of my civic duty to feed the occasional prisoners.'

'I'm in your debt, ma'am. It sure enough feels like my brisket is nailed to my back-bone, and I think my throat is lined with limestone.'

She hesitated only a moment, then came over to where he was seated. Bound in

chains, he was not likely to grab and over-
power her.

'My name is Cora Ankers. I'm told that
you are Ranz Tanner.'

'Yes, ma'am.'

He took the offered plate and set it on the
ground. When she handed him the cup, he
took several big swallows and drained it
empty. It helped to cut the dust and soothe
his parched throat.

'Ah! That's the best drinking water I ever
tasted, Miss Ankers. It is "Miss," isn't it?'

She gave her head a curt nod and reached
out and took the cup. 'I'll fill it again. There's
a water bucket for the guard right outside.'

'Got myself a chaperone and everything,
huh? Folks are keeping a sharp eye on me.'
He laughed without mirth. 'They must have
believed everything old Joe said about me.'

Her expression took on a stern look.
'You're a killer, aren't you?'

He picked up the plate and dug the fork
into the beans. Then he looked up and said,
'That's what Joe says.'

'Do you deny it?'

'Let's just say that Joe could turn a dust
devil into a full-blown tornado with the
extra wind he adds to his tales.'

'Then, you didn't kill three deputies?'

'I've done a few questionable things in my time, but I ain't never drawed down on a lawman, Miss Ankers.'

Cora studied him awhile, and then placed the lamp on the floor and went out of the small room. She soon returned with a water bucket.

'The guard can always get more water,' she said. 'It's extremely hot and muggy in here.'

He couldn't help watching as she opened the top button of her collar to allow herself a bit more air. She caught his look and realized what she was doing. She jerked her fingers away from the collar and showed a trace of pink in her cheeks.

'Why were you sentenced to Yuma?' She seemed eager to turn his attention elsewhere. 'Are you a thief or bandit of some kind?'

'You write the local gossip or something?'

She frowned. 'I was trying to make conversation. I thought you might be lonesome for company and some small talk. Joe can't be much fun to listen to for days on end.'

He grinned, wishing he had been allowed to shave. Covered in dust and unshaven, he must look like a pretty desperate criminal.

'You were right about me right off, ma'am. I'm here because I killed a man.'

That news rocked her. In fact, she took an

involuntary step back from him.

'You actually killed a man?'

'His luck had run out.'

'And what about *your* luck?'

Ranz lifted his shoulders in a shrug. 'If I'd been the one killed, he wouldn't be here in my place. My luck has always been bad, but my speed and aim with a gun were always above average.'

'I don't believe in good or bad luck. I think men and women make their own kind of luck.'

He forked another bite of food into his mouth. The taste was far superior to anything Joe had been feeding him lately.

'Well, aren't you going to dispute my assessment?' she said.

He thought for a second. 'Depends.'

'On what?'

'On what "dispute" and "assessment" mean.'

That put a knowing look on her face. 'You aren't educated.'

He didn't care for the manner of her speech. 'Education ain't always doing book learning or being able to handle numbers.'

'Is that so?'

'Take the Apache, for example. They can read sign like it was a book. They never got no schooling, but they can live off of grubs or roots that would make a white man sick. A handful of them have been running our trained and educated troops ragged since the end of the War Between the States. We out-number them twenty to one and have a heap more schooling than they do. Still, we can't whip them.'

'I suppose there's something to be said for a practical education, same as a proper one.'

'Me, I never had no proper learning. My father worked tending bar, and my folks needed me to plow and look after the fields. I had to help feed six younger brothers and sisters from the time I was old enough to walk.

'Come the war, I joined up with the South. I didn't know what the fighting was all about, but we lived in Louisiana and it was the patriotic thing to do. I lied about my age, being that I was only fourteen, and went off to kill my countrymen.

'Once the war was over, I couldn't find no work. I never had no mind to go back home, so I ended up running horses and cattle across the Mexican border to Emperor Max-imilian.' He paused. 'Wasn't till I got to know some of the locals that I realized that I was on the wrong side. I ended up in a Mexican stockade and nearly got my neck stretched.

'I got away and slipped back to Texas. Landed me a job hazing maverick cattle for a small outfit, and worked up to being a partner. Then we got in a running fight with a couple of big cattle ranchers and I lost my stake. I had to start over from scratch.

'For a time, I hired on to a Basque sheepherder, but some cattlemen drove his herd of sheep over a cliff and killed him. Those fellows put a slug in me too, but I recovered.' He let out a lengthy sigh.

'It seems that every time I hitch my team to a wagon, that there wagon gets burned or wrecked. You say you don't believe in bad luck, but I say it can happen.'

'And what about the man you killed?' Cora asked. 'Do you have an excuse for taking another man's life?'

He didn't care for her superior tone of voice. She probably thought that he was making excuses for ending up in a prison wagon.

'It's real simple, ma'am. I stuck my beak in where it didn't belong. The fellow was giving a young Mexican girl a hard time, but maybe he wouldn't have done her any real harm. I should have turned my back and walked out instead of taking up for her.'

'Fighting over a woman,' she said, showing her distaste. 'Men can be vulgar animals sometimes.'

'Could hardly call that little gal a woman yet. She was no more than fourteen years old.' He watched her closely. 'I doubt that I'd have had to stick up for a woman like you. You being educated and all, I'm sure you could have handled the situation just fine.'

Her face muscles tightened, and her eyes glowed with a spark of anger. She took up the lamp and went back to the door. He knew that he'd stuck his hoof into it with that remark. She stopped at the entrance, framed against the evening dusk.

'Good night, Mr. Tanner. I'll leave you to your conscience.'

'I'm beholden to you for bringing food and water, Miss Ankers. It shows that your heart is in the right place.'

He couldn't make out any change in her expression, but he thought she was going to speak once more. As if thinking better of it, she left the smokehouse, and the heavy door closed. The room became as black as the bottom of a tar barrel.

Ranz, you silver-tongued devil, you're about as handy at talking to a woman as a pig trying to float on its back, he thought.

34

Chapter Four

Stocker bought a bottle of whiskey and waited for Cora to finish her work at the boardinghouse. From his table in the bar, he could watch the building across the street. The place had closed up an hour ago, and yet Cora was still cleaning it. Sometimes it seemed that she took longer than necessary to get her chores done. If he had been a suspicious sort, he might have figured that she was trying to avoid his company.

He spent an hour brooding, constantly sipping the hard liquor. He became surly and irate. He flexed his thick shoulders and looked around the bar for some diversion.

The bar was fairly crowded because Joe Brady was there. He was the biggest liar in the Territory, but all the townspeople gathered to listen to his tales. Stocker supposed that it was understandable, as Joe was the only entertainment around. Even so, it grated on Stocker's nerves that so many men would pretend to believe Joe's every word.

Casting a hard look toward the café again, Stocker felt a renewed surge of rancor. Cora was mopping the place, and that was not her job. He knew for a fact that one of the local women went in early every morning and cleaned the kitchen for her. Cora was purposely stalling.

After storming out of the bar, Stocker planted his bulky frame in the middle of the street and swore aloud. Then he threw his bottle with all his might.

The whiskey bottle crashed into the café window and both of them shattered. Cora dropped her mop and ran out the door. When she spotted Stocker, she slid to a sudden stop.

'Are you crazy?' she demanded. 'What's the idea of breaking my window?'

The noise had attracted a number of men from the bar, but Stocker didn't give a hang about any of them. He crossed toward Cora with deliberate steps.

'You think you can toy with me and dangle me on a string, don't you?' His voice was thick from drink. 'You're the most handsome woman in town, and you dang well like to use it to tease and torment us men.'

Cora took a step back from him. She shook her head. 'I don't know what you're talking about, Stocker. You've had too much to drink. You're not making sense.'

'I'm making sense all right!' Stocker fired back. 'It's time I broke you to harness, you little wildcat.'

Before she could escape, Stocker caught hold of her arms. In front of a dozen men, he pulled her against his chest. His lips sought hers, but she turned her head and avoided contact.

'Stop it! Let me go!' she cried.

But Stocker was lost to his drink and unleashed fury. He wrestled her around the corner of the building and into the alley. There he shoved her against the wooden planks of the wall.

'Fight me if you want,' he slurred through his drunken lips. 'I don't care. Tonight I'm going to kiss you until you're mine.'

An icy fear swept through Cora. She was terrified of the strong brute. When he again tried to press his lips to hers, she turned her head again and cried for help.

In the doorway of the bar, a man shouted at Joe Brady, 'Do something! You're the law, Joe!'

'Yeah, do something, Joe!' another man called. 'You can't let Stocker assault that gal.'

'She's in trouble. You've got to help!' a

third added. 'What kind of lawman are you?'

Joe sucked up his gut and set his hat squarely. His big mouth had done all his fighting in the past, but this was different. He had to stand up to Stocker MacDermit, son of the most powerful rancher in the Territory. As his liquor ran a stream of false courage through his veins, he hitched up his gun and strode out of the bar and over to the alley.

'Let the woman go, Stocker!' he ordered. 'There's law in this here town tonight.'

Stocker had been holding Cora against the wall of the building with such force that she could not breathe. When he turned on the deputy, she fell to the ground, gasping for air.

'Don't mess with me, Joe. I'm not in the mood for any of your blowhard playacting.'

The men had followed after Joe, and their number gave him courage. He confronted Stocker like a queen's champion back in the days of chivalry. Pointing a finger at him, Joe used a strong, booming voice of authority:

'I'm ordering you to get out of town, young MacDermit. You're drunk.'

Stocker's face twisted and grew red from his rage. Taking an ominous step toward Joe, he curled his lips back into a sneer.

'Get outta my sight, Joe! Get outta here before I tear your head off and shove it down your throat!'

'Don't let him push you, Joe!' one of the men called out.

'Yeah, who does he think he is? You're the law!'

'Tell him, Joe.'

The support puffed up Joe's spirits. He placed his hands on his hips and glared at the rancher's son. It was time that someone put Stocker in his place.

'You've been riding high-and-mighty for a long time, Stocker. If you think you can ride over me, you're mistaken. Get out of town and sober up. Get out before I throw you out!'

That was all it took, and Stocker came at Joe with fists flying. The two men locked bodies like two bighorn sheep. They clashed with a flurry of punches, each giving and taking punishment.

Stocker was drunk and Joe was out of shape. The match should have been even, but Stocker wasn't used to taking some of his own punishment. After taking a punch to the eye that knocked him down, he pulled out his skinning knife.

'I'm going to gut you like a butchered hog,

39

Joe! I'll skin you a new hide!'

Joe backed away and grabbed his gun. He pulled it and took aim as Stocker got to his feet.

'Hold it, Stocker. I've got you covered.'

'You're nothing but hot air, Joe.' Stocker came at him a step at a time. 'You ain't nothing. When I cut you open, you'll pop like a balloon.'

Joe looked for help, but the men had all backed off. There was no encouragement now. They were leaving it all up to Joe.

'Grab him!' Joe shouted, taking a step backward. 'Come on, you men. Don't make me shoot him!'

'Run for your life, Joe,' Stocker sneered. 'Run before I get to you.'

In a helpless panic, Joe backed away several more steps. His eyes were wild, searching for help or direction. Stocker kept coming. He could not be stopped. In utter desperation, Joe pulled the trigger.

With a heart of lead, Duke listened to Mouse Davis, the town gossip, snitch, and weakling. He told the story of Stocker's death for a second time.

'And the town?' Duke said afterward. 'They stood there and watched my boy get killed in cold blood?'

'No one tried to interfere, Mr. MacDermit. They egged the two into a fight, but ain't a one of them come forward to stop it. Joe asked for help against your boy, but he didn't get it.'

Duke's shoulders bowed under the heavy weight of his sorrow. He could not believe it. His boy was dead, murdered, shot down in his youth. Stocker would never again ride at his side, never ramrod the Circle M. There would be no grandchildren, no retirement from running the ranch, no one to spend his twilight years with.

'So that's the way it happened?' Duke kept his voice strong, swallowing back the sob that lodged in his throat.

'Every word, Mr. MacDermit. The Ankers girl was cussing your boy and calling for help. Joe come out with the others to see what was going on. That's when the guys started pushing him to do something.'

Duke clenched his teeth in hate. 'And they let an unarmed man be killed? They just sat back and watched?'

'Well, your boy did pull a knife. He threatened Joe.'

'Then Joe killed him.'

'It happened about that way,' Mouse reported. 'Stocker had been doing a lot of drinking, Mr. MacDermit. I reckon that was what drove him to try and kiss the gal right there in front of all those people. He was mad about her keeping him waiting longer than necessary. I heard him say something to that effect.'

'Joe never gave him a chance,' Duke concluded. 'He gunned him down like a mad dog.'

Mouse's skinny shoulders drooped. 'Joe called to the other men to grab your boy and take away the knife. But no one offered to help.'

'You let me know what else you hear, Mouse. I'll be in for my son's body. When is the hearing going to be for Joe?'

Mouse hesitated. 'There won't be no hearing. Joe is the only law in town. He was acting as a lawman at the time. Far as I know, that's the end of it.'

Duke held his temper in check. 'No hearing, huh?' He grunted contemptuously. 'So that's their game.'

'The mayor is figuring to bring your boy's body out to you in the morning.'

Duke shook his head. 'Tell Gus that I'll be in to pick my boy up myself. I don't want to be owing favors to no one.'

'Sure thing, Mr. MacDermit. Whatever you say.'

Duke reached into his pocket and pulled out a gold piece. He flipped it into the eagerly awaiting hands of Mouse Davis.

'Thanks for coming out, Mouse. Keep your ears open for anything I ought to know about.'

'Thanks. Thanks a lot, Mr. MacDermit. You bet. You can count on me.'

Duke watched him ride out of the yard. Con Velarde had been listening from the next room. He entered at once and stood alongside the Cross M owner. Regret was deeply etched in his face.

'What a crying shame, boss,' he said softly. 'Your boy was a mite wild, but he was all man. I, for one, am really going to miss him.'

Duke tried to blink away the tears in his eyes. 'Have a wagon ready at first light. We'll go into Adobe Wells and pick up my son...'

'Sure thing, boss. You want any of the other men to ride in with us?'

Duke stared off into space for a while. Then he took a deep breath and drew on his inner strength. He pounded his right fist into the palm of his left hand. There was fire in his eyes and rancor in his voice.

'Round up Locker, Stringer, and Keats. I

want to talk to them right now, this minute! When we ride into town, it'll be for more than retrieving my boy's body.' His voice grew cold and full of venom. 'I let those sniveling cowards squat in my valley! For my son's sake, I let them steal my cattle and my land. Well, Stocker is dead. They helped to kill him. Now they're going to pay the price!'

Con didn't question what Duke had in mind. He had learned that obeying orders without question was something Duke admired. He left the house to gather the men. He didn't relish the idea of waking them up in the middle of the night, but there were things to be done.

Duke strode into the living room and slumped into his big easy chair. He put his face into his hands and felt the wetness of his tears.

'And blast you too, Stocker!' he said, his voice cracking with emotion. 'You big dummy! No woman is worth getting killed over. What was so all-fired great about Cora Ankers?'

For a few minutes, grief held him in its grip. He had never cried in his life, never shed tears of sorrow. He'd lost a wife to fever and two kids to chicken pox and an Indian arrow, but he'd never broken down and bawled like a baby.

To lose Stocker was different. He was the only child to measure up to his standards. He recalled his son's saying it right out earlier that night – they were two of a kind. He had nailed the truth of the matter square with that remark. They had been cut from the same bolt of cloth, cloth of a unique pattern.

He had known that Stocker was wild and full of vinegar, but it was something the boy would have outgrown in time. He had had the makings of a great man. He would have come around. They would have run the Cross M together, riding side by side.

All of Duke's dreams for the future were dashed to bits. He had even planned the location of Stocker's home, a short distance from the main house. He could walk over in the evenings and bounce his grandsons on his knee. Stocker's wife would cook their Sunday dinner and he and his son would get together after the meal. They would sit on the porch and drink a little, maybe smoke a pipe or evening cigar, and discuss the business of the ranch.

He had not built the empire for himself.

He had dreamed of having Stocker at his side. Everything he had done had been with the thought of his son in mind. Tonight, the town had stood back and let some wandering, big-talking deputy kill him.

They would not stop the fight. He remembered Mouse's words. *Joe had called to the townspeople to help, but they did not interfere. They let Stocker be killed.*

'Blast their yellow hides!' He snarled the words aloud. 'I gave them the land and water. I let them live on my land. And this is my payment!'

Duke knotted his gnarled knuckles into tight fists. He pounded on the arms of the chair with a mixture of rage and grief.

'That's the end of it!' he vowed. 'They'll pay for this. They'll pay with their lives!'

Chapter Five

Ranz was puzzled at pulling out before sunup. The wagon wheel had not been repaired and breakfast was forgotten. He had been hustled out to the iron cage and shoved inside.

'What's all the rush, Joe? One of the women in town threaten to marry you?'

'Put a button on your lip, Tanner. I ain't got no time for jawing. We're heading for Yuma.'

Ranz was glad that he had been left some water by the woman who fed him the previous night. He had drunk until he felt his stomach would explode. The refreshment and rest had left him feeling pretty good ... under the circumstances.

The horses were hitched with haste and Joe was up on the wagon seat at once. Then he was driving them out of town at a brisk pace. Ranz was silent for a time, but then he moved up to a position next to the front of the cage.

'What's the matter, Joe? You get caught

cheating at cards, or what?'

'Shut up, Tanner. I don't want none of your mouth today.'

But Ranz did not let up. 'What about that black eye of yours? Was that from a man or a female?'

'You never learn, do you?'

'I don't get around much, being jailed in a smokehouse. Can't blame me for being curious.'

Joe slapped the reins on the rumps of the horses and picked up the pace. The wagon bounced so violently that it was hard for Ranz to speak. He decided that he would have to keep to himself and pick on Joe later.

They did not get far. Approximately three miles out of town, two men blocked the road and forced the wagon to stop. Ranz leaned against the bars and tried to see what was going on.

'Trying to sneak out on us, Joe?' one man asked. 'I'm real surprised at you. I always figured that a man who talked as big as you would never run from anyone.'

'I've got a schedule to maintain,' Joe replied. 'Get outta the way, Keats.'

Ranz pressed against the bars and could see the one called Keats. At his side was a

48

dark man with an odd sort of smile on his lips.

'You must be pretty fast with your iron,' the smiling man spoke up. 'I've heard about you and your tall tales.'

Joe was sweating. 'Look, fellas, I got to get this prison wagon moving. I've got a schedule to keep.'

'Duke would like a few words with you,' Keats said. 'He has a few questions concerning what happened last night. I know you'd be only too happy to tell him your side of the story.'

'Sure, sure.' Joe wiped his forehead with the back of his hand and removed his hat. As he brought the hat down, his other hand was slipping up to grab hold of his gun.

It was an old trick. Cover your gun hand while you draw. It was so old that the smiling man knew exactly what Joe was doing. When Joe jerked his pistol, he was about one second too late.

The gun blast startled the horses, but Keats grabbed the lead horse and held them. The other man held his gun steady, watching Joe fold over on the prison-wagon seat.

'Guess he won't be talking to the boss after all, Keats. I knew he'd try to get the drop on us.'

'He didn't reckon with the likes of you, Con,' Keats said. 'Looks as if another man has died under your gun. Con Velarde, fastest man with a gun in the whole territory.'

Con's smile faded. 'Wish I had been in town last night. Things would have turned out different.'

Keats seemed to notice Ranz for the first time. He let go of the horse's halter and rode back to look him over.

'You're a witness,' he pointed out. 'Just what did you see, mister?'

Ranz was not sure of the right words. If the two men wanted, they could pin the murder on him. A bullet in him, a gun by his side, and it would look as if he and the deputy had shot it out between them. And so he said:

'From my point of view, Joe tried to draw on the two of you. He wasn't near so quick as your friend. I'd have to call it self-defense. Of course, who would take the word of a convict?'

Con rode up alongside of Keats. He smiled at Ranz, but there was no sign of friendship in his expression.

'What's your handle, fella?'

'Ranz Tanner.'

'What did you do to end up in a prison wagon?'

'I killed a man in a fight. He had more friends than I did.'

Keats laughed. 'Sounds like you drew cards in a hand where the deck was stacked.'

'Did that for a fact.'

Con's wry simper never wavered. 'A man could die in that prison wagon. What should we do with you?'

'Guess you have the options there,' Ranz replied carefully. 'I'm not much of a threat in these irons and locked in this cage.'

Keats nudged his horse to the rear of the wagon. He drew his gun and aimed at the lock. The blast of his gun spooked his horse. It danced about a few steps, then settled back down.

'You're a free man, Tanner,' Con said in a silky-smooth voice. 'Take that body back to Adobe Wells. Mr. MacDermit would want the people there to know that Joe Brady has been killed.'

'Whatever you say,' Ranz responded.

The two men jerked their horses about and rode off in a cloud of dust. As soon as they were gone, Ranz climbed out of the wagon. He got the keys from Joe's pocket and removed his wrist and leg irons.

Sitting atop the prison coach, he wondered if he was doing the smart thing by going back to Adobe Wells. If he pushed on ahead, he could likely outdistance any pursuit. He might make the next town and turn over the body of Joe Brady. He could also turn himself in and complete his trip to Yuma.

'What do you think, Ranz?' he asked aloud. 'You've never made a right decision in your life. Do you think you can do it this time?'

After considering his alternatives, he took up the reins. He knew that the wagon wheel would not withstand hard travel. If he had to run from MacDermit's gunmen, he did not wish to do it on a crippled wagon. He would let Keats call the shot and head for town. If it was the wrong decision, at least he could blame it on someone else.

Cora had not slept during the night. She felt responsible for Stocker's death. For hours on end, she had blamed herself for the fight that left him dead. She kept thinking that she should have handled things differently.

If only I hadn't kept him waiting so long. Maybe he wouldn't have gotten drunk to the point of not using his head. Should I have submitted to his advance? That would have saved his life too.

But she could not lie to herself. She had never invited the attention that Stocker always gave her. He had chased after her constantly, but never had she responded to his coarse and often drunken overtures. The entire romance was one-sided. He would not take no for an answer, and she could never bring herself even to like him.

Again and again, she relived the events of the evening. She was responsible for a man's death. It didn't seem possible. Stocker claimed that she teased men, that she used her looks to drive them crazy. She would have laughed at that if not for the dire situation. Why did she pick clothes that hid her attractive features? Why did she never apply any rouge to her lips or cheeks? Why did she pull her long and silky brown hair into unflattering buns at the back of her head? She had constantly gone out of her way to dull her appearance and try to look plain.

Under all of her poise and outward calm, she was haunted by memories. She had suffered undeserved punishment from her stepbrother. It was something she could not put out of her mind.

Cora closed her burning eyes. She rubbed the lids lightly, knowing that the discomfort was from lack of sleep and not from any thought of crying. She could not bring herself to cry over the likes of Stocker MacDermit. He had been a bully, an arrogant, cruel, and worthless human being. The only respect he had ever been shown by the people of Adobe Wells had been evoked by fear.

By the same token, she had not wanted him dead, and she had expected him to lose interest in her eventually. After doing her best to rebuke his every advance for months on end, she had hoped that he would turn his attention to another woman.

The riders entered the street five abreast. Cora backed away from the window of her room. She could still see the men in the street, but it was unlikely that anyone could see her.

She recognized the men from the Cross M. There were Locker, Stringer, Keats, Velarde, and the king of the roost himself, Duke MacDermit.

They rode up to the mayor's store and waited. When Gus came out to meet them, Cora moved a little closer, trying to pick up their words.

'I would have brought Stocker out to you, Duke, but Mouse said that you were coming in for him. I laid your boy out in the back of my wagon. Feel free to take it to your ranch.'

Duke nodded to Stringer, who rode around to the rear of the store. There was a profound silence until he reappeared. He was sitting on the wagon and had tied his horse to the tailgate. He guided the team of horses up to the four other riders and stopped in the middle of the street.

Duke took a long look at the covered body. Then he fixed his gaze on Gus and yelled, 'I'm giving you fair warning, Mayor. I want you all out of my valley by noon tomorrow.'

Cora heard the words, but it took a second for it to dawn on her what the man had said. She stared aghast, able to see that the news had hit Gus equally hard.

'What are you saying, Duke?' Gus's voice was hoarse. 'We live here. We've made our homes–'

'You stood by and let my boy be killed!' Duke roared, his shoulders shaking with rage. 'I know that Joe asked you to intervene, to help him against my boy. You and the rest of these spineless coyotes stood back and did nothing.'

'Stocker had a knife, Duke! What were we

supposed to do against him?'

Duke was not of a mind to argue. 'You heard me, Gus. I want everyone out of my valley. If you're still here at noon tomorrow, you'll get leveled with the rest of the town. I'm going to burn Adobe Wells to the ground. Any man, woman, or child who remains will be buried in the ashes.'

As the wagon and four other riders left town, Cora watched with unseeing eyes. Fear swelled up within her chest, and terror tore at her heart with icy claws. Duke MacDermit meant to destroy her boardinghouse, her whole world! The words kept ringing in her ears like echoes from canyon walls: *I'm going to burn Adobe Wells to the ground!*

Ranz could see the main street of town. He held back the team, maintaining a slow, steady approach. The wheel was so loose that it was rolling cockeyed. If he hurried the wagon in the slightest, the axle would be dragging in the dirt. He was surprised to see the entire population of Adobe Wells gathered on the Street ahead.

As he approached, someone shouted and pointed in his direction. He continued toward them until he pulled up even with the general store.

'What happened?' the mayor was the first to ask.

Ranz tipped his head toward the prison cage. 'A couple of fellows stopped us on the road out of town. One of them – man named Velarde – shot it out with Joe. You can see who won.'

That brought a lot of mumbling among the crowd. Ranz swept over their faces and saw a mixture of shock, fear, and dread. Women had their arms about their children, and the men had long expressions.

'Why did you come back?' a woman's voice broke the silence.

Ranz looked around until he spotted the lady who had brought him food and water. It had been Cora Ankers speaking.

'I don't intend to have a murder and escape charge added to my time, ma'am. I brought Joe here so that there would be no mistake about who killed him.'

Gus nodded. 'You did the right thing, Tanner. We'll look after the body.'

'What's the gathering for?' Ranz had let his curiosity get the best of him. 'Somebody else die?'

'You don't know?' Gus asked.

'Know what?'

'Joe killed Stocker MacDermit last night.

Shot him dead.'

'He sentenced us all to death!' a woman cried. 'Duke is going to kill us all!'

That brought a flurry of other oaths and woes, but Ranz couldn't sort them out. He frowned in confusion until Gus raised his hands for silence and said:

'Hold on! Keep your wits about you. This is no time for panic. We've got to make some hard decisions.'

'I don't get it, Mayor,' Ranz said. 'What's happening here?'

'It don't concern you, Tanner. If you know what's good for you, you'll take one of the team from that prison wagon and ride out. Turn yourself in at Yuma and serve your time.'

'About my sentence, I...'

'This isn't your fight, Mr. Tanner,' Cora spoke up again. 'It would be best for you to leave as quickly as possible.'

'Wait a minute!' a young man cried as he pushed through the crowd. 'I know about Ranz Tanner. I done heard about him killing Cully Noonan in a gunfight. My cousin was with a trail herd down that way. He told me all about it. We could use a gun like his.'

Gus held up his hand as people began to argue about taking up with a convicted criminal. He shouted all of them to silence.

'First things first,' he said, looking over each man in the crowd. 'We haven't decided what's to be done yet.'

'I say we fight!' the young man spoke up again.

'Easy for you to say, Jess,' another man took up the challenge. 'You don't have a family to think about. We've got to think of the women and children too. I don't want my kids or wife injured or killed.'

'You gonna crawl out of town, Flanders?' Jess fired back. 'You going to tuck your tail and run like a scolded pup?'

'You've got only yourself to think about, Jess. I've got to think of my family!'

'Quiet down, both of you!' Gus roared. 'Let's not start squabbling among ourselves. We need to decide what we're going to do as a group.'

'A vote!' Jess shouted. 'Let's take a vote!'

But Gus folded his arms stubbornly. 'Let's first consider whether we're goin' to fight or leave.'

Ranz did not know where the informal meeting was headed, but he figured to stick around long enough to find out where he stood. He could ride out if he didn't like their decision. After all, he had a date in

Yuma that would clear his name. That was the most important thing he had to do in the near future.

'The Cross M has thirty riders and several thousand head of cattle,' Gus pointed out. 'They can stampede those cattle through town and then burn it to the ground. With his army of men, we haven't much of a chance in a fight against Duke.'

Gus let that settle in, then continued: 'Also, I've taken a quick tally of our strength, and here are some numbers for you to think about. We've eleven women and twenty-five kids to think about. Of the eighteen men in town, two are well along in years and one is blind. Of the other fifteen, not more than six served in the war. The Cross M has thirty hard men able to ride and shoot. Add to that, they have Con Velarde, and our chances look pretty slim.'

Cora spoke up first: 'Yes, but we have our homes here. Everything I own is here. My boardinghouse is my life. I have flowers and a garden. I don't consider Adobe Wells just a town. It's my home.'

Her statement was cheered by a number of people. Gus held up his hands to stop bickering and arguments that broke out once again. He cried out:

'All right, all right! Everyone knows what we're up against. I think we should vote on whether to stay or leave. Naturally, if the vote is to stay and fight, it won't be binding on anyone who's set on leaving.'

Gus pulled out his timepiece. 'Five minutes, and then we take a vote. Each family must make its own decision.'

The people spoke among themselves, each family making up its own mind. Ranz sat by and waited. He was mildly curious when Cora came over to stand next to the prison wagon.

'I'm to blame for this,' she said quietly. 'Joe killed Stocker for the way he was treating me. I should have handled it some other way.'

'You saying that it's all your fault?'

'It's wrong to kill a man for no more than Stocker was doing. If I had submitted to him, this wouldn't have happened.'

'That the way it is, huh?' Ranz said, wondering at her peculiar attitude.

'What about you, Mr. Tanner?'

He lifted his eyebrows in surprise. 'Me?'

'Do you think that Duke MacDermit will let you leave?'

'Why not?'

'No one will be allowed to carry word to

the next town. He can't take the chance that you might send word to the nearest fort. The soldiers might take a dim view of his running all of us out and destroying the town.'

'What's to stop all of you from going to the nearest fort and asking for help?'

'It wouldn't matter. By the time we returned, our homes would be ashes and dust. There would be nothing to come back to. I imagine Duke could tell the soldiers that the Indians raided and burned the town to the ground. How could they know who was to blame?'

'And you would still have no homes,' he concluded.

'Yes, we would still lose our homes.'

'Time!' Gus called out. 'Gather about and let's see a show of hands.' He waited until everyone was assembled, then grew deadly serious. 'How many are for leaving town and not taking up arms against Duke MacDermit?'

It stirred something deep inside Ranz, but not a single person raised a hand.

'How many want to stay and fight for what is ours?'

They all raised their hands. It was one of the most courageous things that Ranz had ever seen. Foolhardy, probably, but it showed real grit.

'It's settled,' Gus declared. 'We stay and fight!'

There was a round of cheering. Everyone was geared up to meet the challenge, but against such odds, they had very little hope of winning. All of them knew the risks, and still they were united.

'We need someone to lead us,' Gus suggested. 'Who among us has seen the most combat?'

'Old Henry!' Jess said with a wry grin. 'Just listen to him at the bar on Saturday night.'

Henry was a thin and frail-looking man, past sixty years of age. A shock of white hair showed from under his Yankee cap, and he could have been blown off his feet by a strong sneeze. He grinned broadly at the mention of his name.

With a hand on Henry's shoulder, Gus said, 'We all know that Henry was a holy terror in his prime, but we need someone with some recent experience. This is going to be a war, and we have to prepare for it. If we are to have any chance against the Cross M, we need to be organized into a smooth fighting unit.'

There was a long silence while each man evaluated the others around him. Then Cora raised a hand for attention.

'There's a man here who is amply qualified to take charge of our ranks.' She paused and put her glowing, chocolate-colored eyes on Ranz. 'This is the man we need – Ranz Tanner!'

It was only his knees that kept Ranz's lower jaw from hitting the floor of the coach. He couldn't find any words. Indeed, the woman's words had taken him and the entire town by complete surprise.

'Ranz Tanner served in the War Between the States for three years. He also fought in the war in Mexico and was involved in a range war down in Texas. I would think that he has more experience than anyone else in our town.'

'But he's a convicted killer!' someone objected. 'He's on his way to Yuma. We can't put a man like him in charge of defending our town.'

'Wait a minute!' Jess cried. 'Maybe the lady has something. Ranz is good with a gun and he's got a lot of fighting in his past. Could be that Providence brought him to our town at this time.'

Gus took a step forward and looked Ranz

squarely in the face. 'What do you have to say, Tanner? You don't have to fight with us, but there's a good chance that Duke and his boys won't let you leave the valley alive. In a war of this sort, you're pretty much forced to take one side or the other.'

'I hate to be a wet rain on your fire, Mayor, but I don't have any reason to join your cause. I don't know anything about this feud. I'm on my way to Yuma, remember?'

'Suppose we could get you a pardon, Tanner? I happen to know the Territorial governor personally. He would look very favorably on your lending us a hand.'

Cora swung around to look at him. 'Helping us would serve you better than spending five years in prison. All we need is someone who can organize a defense of our town. You're the practical choice for that chore, Mr. Tanner.'

'I don't know,' he replied. 'I don't have any business in this here fight, and I'm not the kind of guy who looks for trouble.' He glanced over the eager faces. 'I know that some of you don't want me in town, so you'd better think about that too. As for me, I'll give it some serious thought while I get a bite to eat.'

He climbed down and helped another

65

man pull the body of Joe Brady out of the wagon. They carried him into the nearest shop and laid him out on the floor. Then he walked down to the boardinghouse to wait for Cora. He knew that he couldn't get a meal until she and the others were finished arguing back and forth.

He really didn't know if he wanted them to offer him the job. He had nothing to gain by staying for a fight, because he was already promised a pardon. It was a fool's game to stick in Adobe Wells and take up a gun against an army.

On the other hand, these seemed like good people. He didn't know the whole of the story behind Stocker's death, but he figured that the guy had had it coming to him. If Joe had been involved, it must have been something really mean and brutal.

When Cora entered the dining area of her boardinghouse, Ranz was sitting in a chair, contemplating his life and the strange turn of events that had brought him to his present situation. He couldn't read anything in her face. She would have made a good poker player.

'You left without breakfast. I have some cold roast beef, hard rolls, and coffee.'

'That would be fine.'

She went past him and into the kitchen. Within a few minutes she returned with a cup and a plate. She placed the food and coffee in front of him on the table. He took a sip of the coffee before speaking.

'You make a fine brew, ma'am.'

'Thank you, Mr. Tanner. Can I get you anything else?'

'No, thank you, ma'am.'

She sat down across from him and waited. He wondered what she was thinking about. Like a superb cardplayer, she never tipped her hand one way or the other.

'You people decide what you're going to do?'

'You were there when we said we would fight rather than leave our homes. That part should've been obvious.'

'Now for the question of fighting an army of gunmen. What did you choose to do about them?'

Cora took a deep breath. 'I'm to ask for your help.'

He took a bite of one of the rolls. It was light and tasted freshly baked. For a moment he waited for her to continue. When she didn't, he looked hard at her and said, 'And *are* you going to ask me?'

She hesitated, refusing to meet his gaze. 'I

don't feel right about it, Mr. Tanner. I ... I believe I was impertinent and a bit presumptuous by volunteering you. You have no reason to fight for our town. As you so aptly pointed out, this is not your fight.'

'How did you come to be living in Adobe Wells?' he asked, hoping to change the subject completely. 'It's rather odd to find a woman living all by herself out in the middle of nowhere.'

'I came here with my aunt. She had consumption, and this climate is supposed to be good for that. They say the dry air helps.'

'Did it?'

'She died shortly after we arrived. I think she moved here too late to get any benefit.'

'And you stayed on?'

'The boardinghouse was her idea. There is a monthly stage line that comes through, and there was no café or bathhouse. I'm afraid my only steady customer is Old Henry. He gets some money from the United States Army as retirement. If not for him, the place might as well be closed, except for feeding stage passengers one day a month and an occasional traveler.'

'It's tough to be on your own. I've been that way most of my life, and it leaves a lot to be desired.'

'I enjoy the freedom and independence of owning my own business, Mr. Tanner. I don't have to answer to anyone, and I'm part of something that benefits other folks.'

He studied her for a moment. 'You speak as if you are married to this here boarding-house. Is there some reason you don't want a man in your life?'

'Stocker was a man, and he wanted me to be a part of his life. I didn't want what he had to offer.'

'There are other men.'

Something flickered in her eyes, like the tip of a candle's flame. The corners of her mouth became taunt with thin lines.

'Men are not the only thing a woman has to live for, Mr. Tanner. I believe it's possible to have a life without a husband.'

He detected an underlying bitterness, but was careful not to comment on it.

'Everyone needs someone to share their life with, Miss Ankers. I can't speak from ex-perience, because I don't have none. Since leaving home, all I've ever had was a horse. I've been a loner for the past eight years, and it ain't no life for man nor woman.'

'I'm not alone. I have boarders and friends.'

'So you have.' He forced a smile. 'What about the coming fight? You were the one who gave me a hard time for killing a man, but now you're contemplating a battle that will maybe kill thirty people or more – some of them women and kids.'

Cora wrestled with that. It showed in her expression. 'I suppose that some things are worth fighting for.'

He narrowed his gaze. 'Funny sense of worth you put on things, Miss Ankers. I tell you that I killed a man while sticking up for a young Mexican girl, and that's bad. Joe killed Stocker for your sake, and you think that was bad. Yet you're telling me that it's okay for us to kill dozens of people over a little piece of land. Is your boardinghouse worth more to you than your life or your honor?'

She glared at him. 'What do you know about honor? You're a convict, a killer!'

He was taken aback at the vehemence in her voice. More than that, he didn't like her choice of words.

'You've got a fine manner when it comes to asking a man to get killed for your sake, Miss Ankers. I think I'll pick me one of the team for a horse and ride out. If you want to die for this two-story boardinghouse, you go right ahead. My life is worth more than a few wooden planks and a rough shingle roof.'

Ranz rose to his feet, curtly touched the brim of his hat, and started away from her.

'Wait!' she called out as he reached the door. 'Please, Ranz. Don't go!'

He stopped, his hand on the knob of the door. It wasn't the sudden urgency in her voice but her choice of words. He couldn't remember the last time that a woman had called him by his first name.

'I'm sorry,' she said, her voice as soft as the whisper of an evening breeze. 'I ... I don't know why I snapped at you. Maybe...'

He looked over his shoulder at her. Cora was visibly fighting an inner war. It showed in her eyes and in the fact that her words were being chosen with the utmost care.

'You have no reason to help us with our fight. I was wrong to insult you. I ... I beg your forgiveness.'

Something in the way she forced out the end of her sentence intrigued Ranz. It was as if she had never in her life asked anyone to forgive her for anything.

'You don't have to apologize for calling a kettle black, Miss Ankers.' He took a deep breath and let it out slowly. 'I guess a convict and a killer is what I am.'

She ducked her head, hiding her eyes. Once again her voice was soft and childlike:

'It isn't what you are but what you said. You are right, and I'm ashamed to admit it.'

Ranz scratched his head. 'I was right about what?'

'About my thinking more of this house than the lives of innocent people. I won't elaborate, but you were right about the importance of this boardinghouse. It's as important as my very life to me, Ranz. In fact, it's like the only raft in an ocean of killer sharks.'

She had used his first name again. It was more disarming than the holding of a gun to his head.

'I can kind of understand what you're saying ... Cora.'

His use of her first name lifted her eyes. He was surprised to see the slender thread of a smile on her lips.

'Truce?' she asked.

He smiled at her. 'If we can come to terms.'

'What terms are those?'

After rubbing the stubble on his face, he removed his hat. 'I sorely need a bath, a shave, and a place to stay. If I'm going to ramrod this crew of hopeless pilgrims, I should at least look presentable.'

'I'll run you a bath and see if I can find you something clean to put on. I have some clothes that a guest once left behind instead of paying his bill.'

'Could I also trouble you for a room, in case this place is still standing come evening?'

'We were given until tomorrow noon to get out. That means that we should be safe tonight. I'll make a bed for you upstairs.'

As she hurried off into another room, he hoped that she was going to draw his bath. He took a moment to reflect on his decision and the prospect of a coming war.

Did it again, Ranz, he told himself, shaking his head. *Don't know how you manage to walk with both feet stuck into your mouth right to your knees. Taking on this fight will likely be the death of you.*

Chapter Six

Keats stood facing Duke MacDermit. He was the foreman of the Circle M and it was his responsibility to tell his boss what he thought. He knew that some of his information was not going to set well with the old man, but he still had to tell him.

'Con took Joe Brady with a single shot. Some of the guys figure that it evens the score for Stocker.'

Duke glowered at him. 'Which of the men are you talking about?'

But Keats was not a tattler. 'I'm telling you this as your foreman, Duke. You know that I'll back your play with my dying breath.'

'So who ain't got the guts to stand with us?'

Keats shook his head. 'I'm in the middle here. I'll tell you what's up, but until a showdown, you'll have to be satisfied with what I can tell you.'

Duke waved his hand impatiently. 'All right, all right, Keats. I know you're a top-notch foreman. What's the word around the ranch?'

'I've counted heads, and this is how it stacks up. We have fifteen men who have either friends or family in Adobe Wells. We also have a few cowhands who ain't worth beans with a gun. Counting myself, Stringer, and Locker, you have sixteen riders backing you here on the ranch. Con is down on the main trail with two others. They're preventing anyone from going or coming into town.'

'Then that makes nineteen altogether.'

'Plus yourself.'

Duke rubbed his hands together thoughtfully. 'Think the people in town will stick it out and make a fight?'

'There are a few tough hombres in the group, Duke. Several were in the war, and I know of a couple of hotheads who will want to hold their ground.'

'What about the Ankers girl? I want her to pay full price for my son's death. Mouse told me that she was the one who set up the fuss.'

'That's about the way I heard it too. If she had been a little more obliging, your boy would still be alive.'

'I ain't never ordered the death of no woman or child, Keats – not even Indians.

But this is different. I let those people move in and take our water and land. I helped them survive the first year with a good number of my own cattle. I gave and I gave to Adobe Wells. Now they've killed my boy.'

'Stringer is gathering a herd of cattle. I imagine we'll have five hundred head by tomorrow noon.'

'Good,' Duke said. 'That ought to be enough to grind the town into dust. If there's anything still standing, we'll burn it to the ground.'

'Whatever you say, Duke.'

'When this is all over, you can give notice to the men who refuse to ride with us. I won't have a man on my payroll who's afraid of a fight. Too many bandits, Indians, and the like around to have a coward working for us.'

Keats sighed. 'Sure thing, boss. I'll get rid of them once we finish our business in town.'

Duke turned his back and Keats left. He heard the door shut but didn't look after his foreman. It hurt that so many of his crew had refused to fight. Did they ride for the brand or didn't they? Of course, he knew the circumstances that had split his ranks into two groups. Many of them did have friends or family in Adobe Wells. It was unthinkable to attack and kill those people a man was close to.

Duke gnashed his teeth together. He had to keep himself above all trivial sentiment. When he's on a mission of vengeance, a man must become either merciless or useless. He, Duke MacDermit, was not a man ever to end up useless.

Cora heard the door open at the front of the house. Because Ranz was taking a bath, she assumed that the new arrival would be Old Henry. When she entered the room, her heart stopped and a thousand memories and fears flooded her mind. The arrival was her stepbrother, Sidney Bunk.

It was three years since she'd last seen him, but he had not changed. When he looked at her, she felt her skin crawl. His malevolent eyes crept over her with a vulgar familiarity, and his yellow teeth showed in his customary smirk.

'Well, well, I tracked you down at long last,' he said. There was no warmth in his voice, only the usual malice. 'Bet you thought you'd pulled a quick one on Mom and me.'

Cora summoned her strength. She had never been able to stand up to Sidney. He dominated her as a man might a dog. She had felt his brutal hands and had suffered punishment and endless torment when they lived under the same roof. With a supreme effort, she now managed to suppress her fear and revulsion.

'What do you want?'

He gave her a cockeyed sort of grin. 'What, no kiss and hug? What way is that to greet your long, lost brother?'

'Stepbrother,' she corrected. 'And I'll repeat myself a second time – what do you want?'

Sidney chortled deep in his throat. 'Don't tell me you're still holding a grudge against me after all these years?'

'You've tormented me for the last time, Sidney. I'm an adult now. I'm of legal age and I don't intend to let you come back into my life and make it miserable.'

He lifted his brows in total innocence. 'Me? How can you say that?'

'If you didn't hear from my letter to your mother, Aunt Grace died. She's buried in the local cemetery.'

'Yeah, I got the news, Bummer. But you forgot to mention a few things in that letter.'

'Don't call me that horrid name!'

That put a sparkle in his eyes. 'Bummer? You don't like the pet name I gave you?'

'I never did. It's a disgusting nickname.'

He showed mock injury. 'But that's what you were, Cora, a lost lamb, one without any mother of her own. I called you Bummer after bummer lambs. Just like one of them, you didn't have no mommy to look after you.'

'Why are you here?'

A new look entered Sidney's eyes. Cora had seen it many times before. The man was greedy, worthless, and cruel. He had been responsible for many of her emotional scars. Simply being in the same room with him gave her a queasy stomach and cold chills.

'Aunt Grace drew out all her money for this little venture of yours. I recall that she had nearly a thousand dollars.'

'What of it?'

He looked around slowly. 'You've done all right by yourself, Bummer. Where did you get the money to buy this place?'

'You know that it belonged to Grace. She left it to me.'

Again he showed a look of total innocence. 'Oh, you mean that you have a signed will, that everything is totally legal?'

Cora was breathing hard, as if she had been running a long distance. Standing up to Sidney was something she had never been able to do. He was too brutal, too quick to strike at her, and her stepmother had always taken his side. With an outward calm, she went over to a small desk.

'I have the paid bills for all of the work done in building this place. You'll see that Grace had only a few dollars left after we finished.'

'Then this boardinghouse is free and clear, with no bank notes against it?'

She hated the tone of his voice. She knew exactly where his thinking was headed.

'There's no mortgage, but there is also no business. If you noticed, we are not exactly on any main trails.'

'Could be that you'll see a change there. They've hit gold over at Vulture City, and a lot of miners will be coming this way. With the limited water in this part of the country, I'd say that the farming ought to boom along this river bottomland.'

'The land is owned by a big cattleman named Duke MacDermit. He isn't likely to allow any more settlers to come into the valley.'

Sidney showed her his usual smirk. A dark, devilish light danced in his eyes.

'Don't try to lie to me, Bummer. You've latched on to this gold mine and are not of

81

a mind to share the wealth.' He grunted contemptuously. 'Because Aunt Grace didn't like me, you think you have the right to cheat me out of my rightful inheritance.'

Cora felt her temper rise. She remembered the many times Sidney had been mean to her. She remembered how he had often struck her with his fist, twisted her arm, pulled her hair, and even kicked her. He had once tried to sell her to two drunken peddlers, and she'd barely escaped with her life. He had been a poison to her all her life, and it was now time for that to stop.

'This is my home, Sidney. I worked for it. I earned it. Grace left her share of this boardinghouse to me. I won't stand by and let you take half of it.'

He arched a brow. 'Oh?' Then he went on with a cruel simper: 'And just how do you intend to get rid of me, Bummer? I'm your brother. I was Grace's rightful nephew while you were an outsider. If anyone has a right to her inheritance, it's me.'

Cora's fists were doubled at her sides. She was rigid, fuming, yet frightened. She had never stood up to Sidney without taking a beating for it. But this was different. This was her home. Grace had died in her arms. They had been very close. The boardinghouse was all she had, and she'd be darned if Sidney was going to take it from her.

She tried one last approach. 'There's going to be a fight. Tomorrow at noon, there's going to be an attack on this town. If we lose the fight, everything you see here will be destroyed completely.'

He laughed at such a preposterous story.

'I'm telling you the truth, Sidney. Ask anyone in town. I'm surprised that you managed to get through the blockade. Duke MacDermit's riders are probably down the road, stopping all traffic from coming through.'

'I saw three guys in the distance, but they didn't bother me none.'

'Probably because you were alone and coming into town. If you tried to leave, you can bet that they would prevent it.'

'Nice try, Bummer, but it won't work. I'm here to collect my share of Grace's fortune.' He looked over the place once more. 'If you want to give me five hundred dollars, we'll call it square. You can have the boarding-house and I'll ride out.'

'Five hundred dollars? Where would I get that much money?'

He shrugged. 'Get a loan at the bank if you haven't got that much stashed away. I don't care how you do it, but those are my terms. I only want what's rightfully mine.'

'Get out of here, Sidney!' she shouted. 'Get out!'

But he didn't move. With a sneer on his lips, he took a menacing step toward her. His big fists were knotted and poised. 'I can see you've forgotten how it used to be, Bummer. Maybe I ought to give you a reminder.'

Cora held her ground, but she knew Sidney wasn't making an idle threat. He had hurt her many times before, and he would enjoy hurting her again.

Ranz looked in the mirror and smiled. *By jingo, there was a human being under all of that dirt and hair. How do, fella. The name is Ranz Tanner.*

He donned the corduroy pants and tan shirt that Cora had laid out for him. The fit wasn't great, but it beat the soiled duds he'd been wearing for the past week.

With his hat and boots brushed off, he looked passable, and he decided that he had better get a move on. There wasn't a lot of time left to organize and carry out any battle plans. He had to round up a gun for himself and then get to work.

He went down the stairs until he heard

voices. Not wanting to intrude, he paused and listened. When he heard Cora shout at someone to get out, he did not hesitate further.

He marched into the living room as a man approached Cora with a cocked arm and doubled fist. The man halted at once as Ranz entered. For a moment, no one said or did anything at all.

Ranz inspected the man. He was about his own size, a bit under six feet, with sandy hair and a thin mustache. He was probably near thirty, with sickly yellow-brown eyes and rotted teeth.

The thing that next caught Ranz's eye was the look on Cora's face. She had paled until she was white, and her eyes were wide and fearful. Before he could speak, she quickly moved over to stand behind him.

'Who's your friend, Bummer?' the man asked.

The man's words sounded degrading to Ranz. He decided right off that he was not going to like him.

'Seems I heard the lady ask you to get out,' Ranz answered for her. 'Are you hard of hearing or maybe just as stupid as you look?'

The man clenched a hand, and his jaw tightened with an instant anger. His yellowish eyes burning, he measured Ranz.

'You don't look like my sister's type, stranger. I wonder if she has grown desperate not to become an old maid.'

His words surprised Ranz, and he turned his head to look back at Cora. It was a mistake to take his eyes off a man like the newcomer. The fist exploded against the side of his jaw and sent him reeling backward. Before he knew he was in a fight, the man hit him twice more.

'No! Stop it, Sidney!' Cora cried.

Ranz got his feet planted and stopped retreating. One eye was about swollen shut, but he still had the other one. When Sidney swung from the heels, he was ready to duck.

May I be condemned to the fiery pits of Hades if I let a man named Sidney whip me! Ranz thought. With a fury, he struck back. He nailed the man square between the eyes and felt his nose crack. He hammered him about the ribs and then jarred several of his teeth loose. Ranz had been in enough fights to know the shortest and surest way to win. He pounded the man and never gave him a chance to hit back.

Sidney tried to cover his face and chest, and he staggered backward. When he hit the door, he clawed it open and tried to run into the street.

Ranz tackled him from behind, and they both landed on the porch. Before Sidney could shake him off, Ranz had the man by the shoulders. With a brutal finality, Ranz slammed Sidney's head against the wooden planks.

'Hit a man that ain't looking, will you?' Ranz snarled. 'Well, take a bite of this!'

He rammed the man's face against the boards once more. Then he got off him and stood up. His chest heaving from exertion, fists ready, he watched to see if Sidney would get up.

But there was no fight left in Sidney. He moaned and turned his head to the side. He spat out blood and crawled away to lick his wounds.

Gus and several others had seen the ending of the fight. There was a noticeable hesitation when Gus approached Ranz.

'Any trouble, Mr. Tanner?'

Ranz did not reply but walked over to the nearest water trough. He ducked his head into the water and then straightened up. With one hand, he brushed his hair out of his eyes. The cold liquid cleared his head at once.

'Are you all right?' Cora's voice reminded

him that she had seen the whole thing. He squinted at her through his one good eye.

'Did he call you his sister?'

A crimson flush colored her face. She lowered her head and her eyes. 'He's my stepbrother. I didn't get along with him and his mother, and I ran away from home. I guess he found out where my aunt and I had moved. He's about the biggest skunk on earth.'

As she looked up at Ranz, he was flattered to see genuine concern in her eyes. 'Come in, Ranz,' she said. 'I'll doctor that cut for you.'

He touched the side of his face and found blood on his hand. He hadn't known about the cut above his left cheek.

'Sidney was wearing a ring,' Cora informed him. 'It tore the skin. I've got some disinfectant.'

Before he followed after her, Ranz turned to Gus. 'Round me up Joe Brady's gun, Mayor. I'll be out to see about organizing the town's defenses in a few minutes.'

'Whatever you say, Mr. Tanner.'

Ranz smiled at the respectful tone of the mayor. When he walked into the boardinghouse, Cora was waiting for him.

'You hear that? The mayor called me Mr. Tanner.'

'It's the least he can do. After all, you're probably going to end up dead on our account.'

He frowned. 'That's a real vote of confidence, Cora.'

She sat him down at the table and got a pan of water and a clean cloth. She dabbed at the cut on his cheek and then doctored it with tincture of arnica. When she had finished her nursing, he grew serious.

'What's the situation between you and Sidney?'

Cora turned her back to him. 'It's personal. I'd rather not involve you in my troubles.'

Ranz got up behind her and put his hands on her shoulders. He was aware that she cringed under his touch and seemed to freeze suddenly.

'If I'm going to get myself killed in the next day or two, I don't see that we should have any secrets. I've told you about my life and about the mistakes I've made. If you have something you'd like to get off your mind, I'd be mighty proud to listen.'

She turned to him, trapped against the sink. There was a mixture of terror and longing in her eyes. It was the most peculiar look Ranz had ever seen.

'I ... I can't talk about it. Really, it's just something that I have to live with. There isn't anything you can do.'

He wasn't about to let her off so easily. 'You watched me beat that stepbrother of yours. You never once cried out for me to stop pounding on him. I might have killed him out there, banging his head on the porch.'

Her head turned from side to side. 'No, you wouldn't do that.'

'I'm a convicted killer, remember?'

She furrowed her brow as if confused and uncertain. 'I – I don't believe that you murdered anyone. I can't believe that of you.'

'Even after seeing me in action?' he asked. 'What about the way I tore Sidney in half? A man gets into a fight and he no longer thinks with his head. He fights on instinct, and my instincts are good.'

Cora didn't reply to that. Instead, she locked gazes with Ranz. There was a depth in her eyes that transcended anything he had ever witnessed. He visualized her insecurity, her apprehensions, her hopes and dreams. For that moment, he was lost within her enchantment.

'I've got to do one of two things,' he said, noting the husky sound of his own voice.

'Either I gather my wits about me and walk away from you, or I take you in my arms and kiss those beautiful lips.'

Cora sucked in her breath and held it. His chest was so close to her that he could almost feel her heart beating. His own heart hammered and he was short of breath, as if there were no air in the room.

'Please,' she murmured.

He had no idea whether that meant for him to leave or to succumb to his impulse. A violent war waged within him. After a long moment he drew up the reins on his feelings.

'Sorry,' he said, releasing his hold on her. 'I don't know what got into me.'

There was a look of relief on her face, but her eyes shone brightly, as if she felt a bitter disappointment. It was about the most confusing thing Ranz had ever come across.

'I'll have supper ready about dusk.' Suddenly Cora was all business. 'Will you be able to eat?'

He regained control of his manners and worked his jaw back and forth. 'Sure. Ain't no man named Sidney going to bust my jaw or knock out my teeth.'

'I – I'm really very sorry, Ranz. I had no idea that he would get so violent with you.'

'I reckon he's more sorry about it, Cora. I'm pretty sure that I broke his nose and loosened some of his teeth. He'll be the one eating soup and mush for a spell.'

'Thank you for coming to my aid. I–'

He did not let her finish. 'Think nothing of it. You don't owe me anything. I'm beholden to you for seeing after me in the smokehouse last night. Could be that we're even.'

'I'll accept that,' she replied, showing a warm smile. 'Let's call our relationship even.'

Ranz left the boardinghouse with a feeling of emptiness. For some odd reason, he didn't like being even. He wanted something more. What that something was escaped him, but the yearning was there.

He had encountered a few women in his time, but he had never been so close to a proper young lady. The idea that he might have been able to kiss her and not get slapped dumbfounded him. He told himself:

Had your chance to toss your rope, Ranz, and you lost your loop. Just like everything in your life, you can't do nothing right!

Chapter Seven

After looking over the town, Ranz drew up a plan for battle. His arsenal included a small amount of dynamite and two barrels of coal oil. Of the fifteen men, he picked the six with war experience and decided to use them as sharpshooters.

Next, he put the women and children to work building a blockade around the perimeter of the town. Wagons, boxes, trash cans – whatever they could find went into the making of the wall. The men were assigned to digging a trench along the main entrance to town.

Ranz supervised and went from place to place. He helped to get rock walls started and took his turn with a shovel. By nightfall, when they had the work about half finished, he ordered a one-hour break and let the people get something to eat and a little rest.

He was pleased to find that, as promised, Cora had left a few minutes early and had his supper on the stove. Equally as pleasant, she had donned a blue-and-white dress. As soft as flower petals, the dress displayed the natural contours of her body and flattered her dark hair and eyes. She had brushed her hair out and it adorned her shoulders in fine silken strands. There was even a hint of rouge on her lips and about her cheeks. She was transformed from quite a plain young woman to one who was nothing short of breathtaking.

'I didn't have much time,' she said, careful to avert her eyes from his. 'I threw together some stew for the three of us.'

Ranz paused a moment to drink in her beauty. It took a real effort to remove his gaze and look around the empty room. 'Where's Old Henry?'

'I haven't seen him since he went to work. You put him in charge of rigging the dynamite charges, didn't you?'

'Yeah. His experience is something we needed.'

She smiled at Ranz. 'I saw his eyes light up when he told me about his assignment. I don't think I ever saw him so eager and excited.'

'Sometimes we forget that older people still have a lot to offer,' Ranz said. 'Youth and energy can make up for a good many things, but those who have lived a long time have practical experience that can't be taught.'

'I remember our discussion about that once before – practical education as opposed to proper education.'

'Both have their uses and worth, I reckon. I'm for thinking I could use more of the 'proper' a good deal of the time. I would have maybe learned something about staying out of trouble.'

'You mean like the job you've accepted here?'

'Is that what you call it – a job?' He smiled at the description. 'Got me a nest of mice fortifying against a pack of hungry wolves. I think I done hitched my team to a wagon loaded with gunpowder. One spark and there won't be enough left of me for the vultures to find.'

'You didn't have to accept the offer.' She was serious, studying him with a curious scrutiny. 'You could have taken one of the team horses and left for Mexico. It will be some time before they start wondering about you at Yuma Prison.'

Ranz didn't reply to that. He dug into the stew and ate a healthy portion. Once he had cleaned his plate to the last crumb, he pushed back from the table. Cora had an expectant look on her face, so he did not disappoint her.

'If you want to know the truth, Cora, I stayed because of you. I expect that there are many good people in Adobe Wells, but you're the reason I threw my ante into the pot.'

She showed an uncertain frown. 'That isn't very sound thinking, to risk your life for someone you've just met.'

It was his turn to take a close look at her. 'Could be right about that, but– Well, you're a lot different from any woman I ever ran into before. I'm for thinking that you're someone very special.'

Crimson darkened her complexion. She tossed her head back, a subtle move to hide her embarrassment.

'That's silly,' she said. 'How can you possibly make such a judgment about me? We haven't been together for more than a few minutes. For all you know, I could be a wicked old witch.'

'I ain't the smartest hombre in the country, Cora, but I do have enough horse sense to recognize a good woman when I see one. I also know that you have no reason in the world to think much of a man like me, being that I'm a convicted killer.'

She bore into him with probing eyes. He

wondered if she was trying to judge him or if she only wanted to believe his flattery.

'I'm not certain what to think about you, Ranz. You could be making fun of me.'

'Only a complete fool would do that. You're a vision of beauty, dressed up neat and tidy the way you are. I reckon there are a good many men who would face certain death for the chance to hold your hand.'

'Looks are not what makes a person,' she said. A wrinkle furrowed her brow. 'It's the intangibles that make a person have worth. Are they caring, compassionate, considerate, of good moral fiber? *That's* what really counts. External beauty can't show what is inside someone.'

'You've already shown that you are made up of those worthwhile things. No one else worried about a low-life convicted killer in that smokehouse. For all you knew, I might have deserved to hang. Everything Joe said about me might have been true. Yet you brought me food and water.'

She squirmed under his gaze. 'I told you that it was my job. I always feed the convicts on the prison wagon. I get paid for it.'

'That might explain bringing a plate of food and a cup of water to the cell. But you didn't have to give it to me personally. You didn't have to get me more water. And you sure didn't have to stick around and talk to me. No, ma'am, there ain't no doubt in my mind. You're a good woman.'

She rose from the table and turned her back to him. He had no idea what she was feeling or thinking. For a while, she appeared to be in deep thought. When she finally spoke, it was more of a murmur, almost as if she were speaking to herself.

'I've never put any faith in a man, Ranz. My Aunt Grace was hurt terribly by a man when she was quite young. He made her a lot of promises and then left her in disgrace. It left emotional scars that never healed. My own father was gruff and often violent. My most vivid memories of the man are of him bellowing in a drunken rage.

'I never knew my mother. My father wouldn't talk about her, and he always got very angry and upset when I asked questions about her. When he remarried, he chose a cold, selfish woman. I had a number of problems with my stepbrother and his friends. After my father died, I was more of a slave or prisoner than a member of the family. Only Aunt Grace treated me kindly. I often thought it was because we had a special insight into each other.'

'Insight,' Ranz said, as softly as his deep voice would let him. He was sure that he and Cora also shared a special insight.

'She knew how it felt to be helpless and alone,' Cora explained. 'She and my stepmother were not on very good terms. She also saw Sidney for what he was – a spoiled and vicious brat.'

Ranz noticed her shoulders droop, as if from under the weight of her confession. Inwardly, he had to wonder why she would bare her soul to a stranger, a convicted killer like him.

'It seems that every man I have known is self-centered, concerned only about his own needs and desires, and thinks that a woman is something to be used and discarded. I didn't simply offer to help Grace move to this land. I ran from my predicament back East.'

'And you blame us men for being good-for-nothings?'

'I know it isn't all men, but ... but I have never known a man that I could trust. My father was cold and bitter, and Sidney showed me a cruel side to men that I can't forget.'

'There are some like him all right, but there are also women who use men for their own greed or purpose and never give a man an even break. We can't condemn a whole bushel of apples because a few have worms in them.'

Cora placed her plate on the counter and slowly pivoted to face him again.

'If we should survive this fight, I would like to sit down and have a long talk with you, Ranz. Maybe I could change my opinion of men. I don't like not trusting half of the world's population.'

He smiled and raised his coffee cup in a toast. 'It's a date. If we live long enough to get the chance, I'd sure love to engage in such a conversation.'

'What's going on, Mouse?' Keats wanted to know. 'Are the townspeople going to pull out or dig in and fight?'

The informant from town looked from Keats to Con Velarde. Mouse Davis was afraid of the gunman. It was as plain as the nose on his face. With a deliberate effort to ignore Con, he spoke directly to the Cross M foreman.

'They're anchored to them pieces of ground like they was staked to them with short chains, Mr. Keats. Ain't no way they can win, but they ain't going to run.'

Keats considered that. 'The boneheaded fools. How do they expect to have a chance against thirty men and a whole herd of cattle?'

'I don't know the whole of it, 'cause there were some in town that didn't trust me. From what I seen, they've put their trust in the convict what came in the prison wagon, a man named Ranz Tanner.'

'What do you know about that, Keats?' Con spoke up. 'We should have left the man in chains. We let him live, and he takes up against us. We might have made a mistake with him. I read some strength in that fellow's makeup.'

'Ranz Tanner, huh?' Keats kept his attention focused on Mouse. 'I never heard of him. You say the people in town are following orders from him?'

'That's right. He's in charge of defenses. I don't know why he took a hand, but the man is trouble for you.'

'What are you going to do now, Mouse? You might have been missed.' Con was regarding the snitch with undisguised contempt.

Mouse cocked his head and gave it a jerk, indicating a pack mule behind his horse.

'Why do you think I've got my goods

loaded? I'm pulling stakes right pronto. Ain't no way that I'm going to be in town when you hit it. I've got me a brother in Texas. Think I'll wander down that way and maybe find a new home.'

'Duke will probably pay you for the information you've brought us, Mouse. He's up at the main house.'

Mouse began to ride past them, but Con reached out and grabbed his horse by the bridle. Fear leapt in the skinny man's eyes.

'I wonder if you might be playing both sides of the fence, Mouse. You wouldn't think of spilling your guts to the first lawman or soldier you bumped into?'

'No, no!' Mouse's voice squeaked from the high pitch. 'I ain't got no call to cross you, Con. I wouldn't!'

'All the same, Mouse, I'd feel better if you stuck around until this is over. A day or two can't matter all that much.'

The weasel was wide-eyed with cowardice. His face twisted into a near-blubbering mien. He looked ready to bawl.

'You can trust me, Con. I ain't never done nothing to backstab you guys on the Cross M. You know that I've always looked out for Mr. MacDermit's interest. I ain't going to tell nobody what you're planning.'

'What do you think, Keats?' Con turned toward the foreman. 'Do you trust this squealing rat to keep his mouth shut?'

Keats thought for a moment. 'You'd best stick around the place until this is over, Mouse. That way, we know you won't be sending out the word for help.'

'You've got me wrong, Keats. I wouldn't turn rat on you guys. What you do to those people in Adobe Wells is your own business.'

'Unless there was a buck in it for you,' Con sneered. 'You'd sell out your mother if there was four bits in it.'

Mouse threw up his hands. 'Let me go!' he cried. 'I'm going to see Duke. He'll let me leave!'

The skinny man kicked his horse and bolted away. His pack mule was not prepared for the hasty start. When his horse hit the end of the lead rope, the mule could not get started quick enough, and Mouse was practically jerked from the saddle as the rope pulled free.

Con's own horse spooked and danced about, but he got him under control and drew down on Mouse. Before Keats could intervene, he fired his gun.

Mouse pitched forward and reeled out of the saddle. He landed hard on his shoulders and head, rolling over onto his back. His horse raced off into the night while the mule trotted behind uncertainly. With no guidance, it stopped a few feet down the trail to munch a stand of buffalo grass.

Keats rode over to Mouse and looked down at his body. 'You didn't have to do that, Con. We could have locked him up until we were finished with the people of Adobe Wells.'

'He'd have gone straight to the law, Keats. You know that a weasel like him don't have no loyalties. Give him a dollar and he'd sing any tune the authorities wanted to hear.'

Keats climbed down and examined the body. There was no recrimination in his voice when he spoke. 'Got him square in the ticker, Con. He never knew he'd been shot.'

'What'll we do with the body?'

'You killed him – you throw some dirt over him. I'll ride to the ranch house and let Duke know what's going on. If that convict is helping the squatters in town, we might have to beef up our attack.'

'What can one man do against us?'

'Depends on the man. There must be some reason they would put him in charge of defending their town. Odd that anyone would let a stranger give orders.'

'Yeah, and who'd trust a man what

stepped right out of a prison wagon?'

Keats looked off in the direction of town. 'Strikes me as a desperate act by desperate people, people on the verge of panic.'

The gunman showed his usual mirthless smile. 'Could be right about that. They're nothing more than a bunch of sheep caught in a prairie fire. They would follow a lion into its den to keep from being scorched.'

'Take care of Mouse's things. I'm riding to the ranch. Keep an eye on the road. We'll all meet at the end of the valley about sunup.'

'It's going to be a bang-up day tomorrow, Keats. I'll be ready for you.'

Keats mounted his horse and started off into the darkness. He felt as if a leaden cloak shrouded his shoulders. Stocker, Joe Brady, and now Mouse Davis. The death toll was mounting.

He fought to keep his conscience clear, but it was a useless effort. He pictured Joe Brady trying to draw against Con. He thought of the fearful expression he'd seen on Mouse's face before he tried to ride away. His mind wouldn't rest. The two deaths were recorded forever in his memory.

Fighting to maintain his composure, he wondered if it would be that way with everyone who was killed. He knew and liked

105

some of the people in town. Old Henry was fun to listen to on Saturday nights. He was always telling those wild tales of the early days in the Southwest territories. Keats would hate to be the man to kill him.

Then there was Gus Fraizer, the town mayor and owner of the only store for a hundred miles in any direction. He also liked Jess Lannigan, the young carpenter, and a few of the others. There were a number of good people living in Adobe Wells.

He kept a good pace toward the ranch while turning over the different faces in his mind. It would be real hard to draw down on some of them. Destroy the town, kill the men, and send the women and children packing – it was a dirty job, no matter how he looked at it.

However, the duty of a foreman was to do the bidding of the ranch owner. He was bound by Duke's decision. He had worked hard to attain his position. Duke had put his faith in him, even over his own son. That was not something to take lightly.

There had been years of riding in other men's shadows, endless months of suffering the cold and heat, eating on the trail, sleeping in wet blankets. He'd fought bandits and Indians alongside Duke MacDermit. For six long years he had worked the Cross M faithfully. He had never questioned an order. When Duke or Stocker wanted something done, he had been the man to see that it was taken care of. Locker and Stringer were loyal and dependable hands, and both had been with the ranch for more than five years. They would stand behind whatever Duke ordered.

But is it right? Keats asked himself. *Can we kill those men and possibly some women and children without question?*

He wrestled with the notion for a long time. When he spotted the lights of the ranch house, he hurried his horse. It did not pay to spend a lot of time dwelling on a decision that had already been made. He rode for the brand. He would follow orders. Whatever it cost him in the future, he was not a quitter. If Duke wanted to level the town of Adobe Wells, he would lead the charge.

Chapter Eight

Most of the people were worn out completely, and Ranz called a halt to the work shortly after midnight. He allowed for two or three hours of sleep. Then the people were to be back on their jobs well before daylight.

Gus met up with him after the groups of workers were dismissed. He gave Ranz the gun and holster that Joe Brady had been wearing. After strapping it on, Ranz took a good look at the mayor. His clothes were sweat-stained and dirty. Etched in his face was a grave and weary look.

'We don't have enough time, Ranz. We'll never have a secure wall up in time. About everything in town is piled in the barricade, but the houses are too far apart. We can't defend it like a circled wagon train 'cause we don't have the manpower or the material to work with.'

'The trench should stop the cattle or turn them, which means that we then will have to handle the riders. There's a chance that they won't want to engage in a gunfight.'

'You don't know Duke MacDermit. He isn't the kind of man to make idle threats. He'll want this place burned to the ground. If we dare to oppose him, he'll want us all dead.'

'It's a little late to change your mind about staying, Mayor.'

Gus puffed up his chest. 'Who said anything about changing my mind? I'm talking common sense. We're in a fix, that's all.'

'Flanders will have the south side of town and Jess Lannigan is on the north. You'll have the rear end and I'll be up front. Sounds like we got all points of the compass covered.'

'Yeah, but–'

'Miss Ankers spoke with the women, and there are seven who can shoot with some accuracy. They can be support-fire for the walls not under attack. That will allow us to move the men to the hot spots.'

Gus sighed. 'Look at the size of this town, Tanner. It must be a hundred yards to either side and twice that from end to end. That's with us pulling in the two outside places to the west and Jess giving up his house to the north. We will lose three homes in the first assault, whether the cattle break through or not.'

'It wasn't my idea to fight, Mayor,' Ranz reminded him. 'You took the vote to stay.'

'Yeah, I know, I know.' Gus wiped his forehead with the back of his hand and looked around once more. 'But you can see how weak we are, can't you?'

'I was with a contingent of Confederates that never won a battle,' Ranz said. 'We were often outnumbered as much as ten to one and seldom had enough ammunition for what few guns we had. Facing long odds is something I'm used to.'

'Then you think we have a chance?'

Ranz laughed at the thought. 'I told you, we never won a battle.'

'You don't offer a man much hope, Tanner.'

'A handful of bullheaded men, several women who have never fired a shot at another human being, and a convict from a prison wagon. Would you put money on an army like that to win?'

Gus appeared confused. 'If that's the way you feel, why stick with us? I'd think that you'd grab a horse and ride out, like Mouse Davis did earlier this evening.'

Ranz frowned. 'Someone pulled out?'

'He was no loss.' Gus snickered his disgust for the man. 'I'll bet you a dime to a good horse that he rode straight to the Cross M and told them everything be knew.'

That gave Ranz some pause to reconsider their situation. 'You really believe that?'

'The man was a sniveling coward, Tanner. Who do you think took word to old man MacDermit about his son? It was Mouse Davis. He was gone as quick as he could saddle his horse. The little weasel would sell everyone he ever knew into slavery for a wooden nickel.'

Ranz reviewed in his mind the lay of the settlement. The most obvious attack point for a herd of cattle was to the front, the west end of town. But if Mouse had relayed the strategy of the town to the men at the Cross M, they might change their plan of attack. It was something to be seriously considered.

'I want a second ditch dug,' he told Gus. 'Soon as you and the others assemble, before daylight, bring tools to the opposite end of town.'

'What for?'

'If Mouse sold us out, the Cross M might attack from that direction. If that happens, I want to be prepared.'

'We already have the coal oil situated to the front of town.'

'Put the barrels on a wagon and keep a

team in harness. We'll have some warning as to the direction of the cattle. Once we know where the stampede is to come from, we'll haul the fuel to that end and get ready.'

'You're giving the orders, Tanner. If that's the way you want it, that's the way we'll do it.'

'Good.'

'One other matter.'

'What's that?'

'There's a stranger in town, the one who gave you that black eye. What do we do with him?'

'His name is Sidney Bunk and he's Cora's stepbrother. I don't know where he stands just yet. From what little I know of him, he won't be on our side.'

'Think he might do the same as Mouse?' Gus scratched his chin.

'We'll keep an eye on him. Where is he?'

'Over at the tavern. He has been drinking off and on, mostly keeping to himself. I don't know where he intends to sleep.'

'Cora explained the situation to him. Maybe you ought to see what his plans are. I doubt that he'd tell me anything other than to drop dead.'

'I'll swing by on my way home. There are only a couple of hours before it'll be time to start again, and I'd like to shut my eyes for at least a few minutes.'

'See you about four-thirty, Mayor.'

Gus hesitated. 'A final word, Tanner.' He cleared his throat and shifted position from one foot to the other. 'I don't know the full reasons for your sticking with us. One man might be able to slip out into the night and get past the guards Cross M has posted.'

'I imagine you're right.'

'It says a lot for your character, deciding to help a bunch of people you don't even know.'

'Yeah, I'm a real prince.'

Gus frowned. 'I'm talking straight here, Tanner. If we come through this, me and some of the others will sign and send off a letter to Yuma. We intend to tell them that you were killed in the fight.'

Ranz felt a swelling of his heart. 'You'd do that?'

The Mayor nodded his head. 'If we survive this battle, you won't have to serve no five years in prison. I thought you'd like to know that.'

'Thanks, Mayor. That means a lot to me.'

The man lifted a hand in farewell and walked away. Ranz went back to the boardinghouse. He could use the sleep too, not that he would get much rest. Facing an impending battle wouldn't lead to any re-laxation, only to an exhausted slumber to recoup strength.

He entered to find a solitary lamp burning on a table. As he crossed the room, he was aware of a shadow that moved. His hand dropped to his gun, instantly ready for trouble.

Cora came into the light and he relaxed at once. She smiled as she saw his reaction.

'We were given until noon tomorrow, Ranz. I don't think Duke would send any of his men in tonight.'

'Could be a change in his plans. A fellow named Davis pulled out this afternoon. From what the mayor tells me, he might have gone straight to the Cross M and told them our plans.'

That put a tight frown on her face. 'What a miserable snake! I never liked that little man, but I didn't think him capable of such treachery.'

'We don't know that he told our plans, but we have to assume that he did. Better not to trust a man who'll turn tail and run in the face of a fight.'

'Have you changed your strategy, then?'

'Not much we can do, regardless of what MacDermit knows. It's no secret as to our strength in numbers, and we can only try to defend the town until he gives up.'

'Or until he wins and burns the town to the ground.'

'There's that possibility too.'

Cora took a hesitant step forward. It put her at arm's length. She did not look at Ranz, but appeared to find a keen interest in staring at the floor.

'I've been doing a lot of thinking,' she murmured. 'This place – this boardinghouse – it isn't worth a lot of people's being killed. Maybe I was wrong to refuse to leave.'

Ranz wondered at her change of attitude. The first time she had spoken about the boardinghouse, it was the most important thing in her life. She had told him that it was the only raft in an ocean of sharks.

'Why the change of heart?'

There was only a dim glow from the lamp, but he could have sworn that Cora was blushing. But that made no sense at all. Why should she be suffering from shame or embarrassment?

She tossed her head and absentmindedly reached up to remove a pesky strand of hair from her eyes. 'Perhaps I have decided that there are more important things in life than owning a business. I don't really know why,

Ranz. I'm ... I'm quite mixed up about the whole thing right now.'

Ranz slowly extended his arms and put his hands on her shoulders. He felt her quiver under his touch. She was trembling, obviously fearful and uncertain. Ever so gently, he drew her closer to him.

'Being scared before a battle is normal,' he said softly. 'Ain't no shame in having those kinds of feelings.'

Her eyes flashed at him. Something in the way she regarded him revealed emotions other than fear of the upcoming fight. She seemed a bit angry that he misunderstood.

'I wasn't thinking of the fight.'

'You're about as shaky as a pair of deuces in draw poker,' he told her bluntly. 'I'd hate to think that it's because you're afraid of me.'

The naked truth sprang into her eyes. She was like a frightened fawn, seeking a direction to flee. He half expected her to jerk out of his grip and dash away.

'In all of my life,' she said in a husky whisper, 'I've never been held close by a man.' She swallowed and ducked her head, almost as if ashamed of the confession. 'Men have pawed at me and tried to kiss me by force, but never have I... have I been in ... in a man's...'

She did not finish the sentence. He slipped an arm around her waist and pulled her against his chest. Instead of doing anything more, he simply held her in that position.

Cora remained apprehensive and shivering within his embrace. She was like a block of ice, firm and unyielding, holding her breath. A lifetime of distrust was not something he could vanquish with a wave of his hand.

'You've nothing to fear from me,' he whispered, his lips close to her ear. 'I would die a thousand deaths rather than do anything to hurt you.'

Slowly, Cora let out her breath and, timorously, seemed to relax. Encircled by Ranz's arms, she finally rested her chin against his shoulder.

They might have been engaged in a very slow and dreamy sort of dance. There was no heated emotion, only a measure of comfort being shared between them.

'So that's the way it is, huh?' a sour, sharp voice shattered the serenity of the encounter. 'You've got your cat claws into a filthy convicted killer!'

Cora sucked in her breath and broke free of Ranz's grasp. Ranz turned sharply, but froze. He stared into the muzzle of Sidney Bunk's gun.

Ranz had the thong off his gun, but he had no chance to draw. Sidney appeared to be drunk, but he had the muzzle of his gun aligned right at Ranz's chest. To make a sudden move was to die.

'Get out of here!' Cora yelled at her stepbrother. 'If you want a fight, wait until MacDermit attacks tomorrow. You'll get all of the fighting you want.'

'I've nothing against MacDermit,' Sidney said with a shrug. 'In fact, I ain't got no reason to get into this fight of yours.'

'You said that you wanted a half share in the boardinghouse,' Cora said to keep his attention. 'Well, if you fight with us tomorrow, you can be half-owner.'

That put a narrow look on Sidney's face. His brows tensed with suspicion. 'Why the change of heart, Bummer?'

'I was wrong earlier today. You were right about Grace being your aunt too. You are entitled to half of what she left me.'

A sneer curled his lips. 'So that's how it is?' He laughed contemptuously. 'You've got your blood all heated up for this worthless killer!'

'We weren't doing anything!'

He glared at Ranz through his swollen eyes. 'I learned about you today, Tanner.

You're a convicted murderer. You escaped from the prison wagon and joined up with these people. Now you've melted our Miss Iceberg. You're really something, killer man. I never figured anyone would find a way to thaw Bummer's frozen heart.'

'A drunk with a gun talks mighty big,' Ranz said. 'You ain't much of a man without an edge. I gave you first punch this afternoon and still fed you a mouth full of porch. You holster that shooting iron and we'll settle this like men.'

Sidney's fist tightened on the pistol. There was a red haze in his eyes, both from drink and a boiling rage.

'I'm going to gut-shoot you, killer man. I'm going to watch you squirm on the floor and die a slow, painful death. We'll see who gets the last laugh.'

Cora stepped quickly between them. 'I won't let you do it, Sidney. You've been mean and cruel to me all my life, but this is where it stops.'

He cocked his gun, keeping a close eye on Ranz. There was no chance to draw. One sudden move and the man would open up on them both.

'I always liked to hear you holler, Bummer. If you get in the way now, I'll put a bullet in you too. Then this boardinghouse would be mine. If the town wins, I could sell it for enough to get a stake.'

Cora was incredulous. 'You're lower than a badger's basement, but you wouldn't shoot your own sister!'

'Stepsister,' he corrected. 'And don't count on it, Bummer. I never liked you, not one bit.' He showed a haughty smirk. 'Do you think I sold you to those peddlers out of love? That was to get rid of you once and for all. They were supposed to tie you up until they found a preacher. Then you would have been forced to marry one or the other and I'd have been rid of you.'

'You had no reason to treat me like dirt. I never did anything to you.'

'Grace used to treat me good until you started growing up. Then it was Cora this and Cora that. She no longer made cookies and taffy for me. They were always only for you. She didn't ask me to spend time at her fine house. It was always you. And when it came time for her to share her wealth, she ran off with you. It's taken me a long time to find you, Bummer. I ain't leaving until I square the account between us.'

Ranz was not going to stand behind Cora. It was obvious that Sidney's melon was not fully ripe. He had the eyes of a lunatic, wide and glassy. One wrong word and he would open fire.

It was too risky to attempt and draw against the man, but the lamp was close by on a table. Without looking at it, Ranz side-stepped from behind Cora. It was an innocent move, as if he were trying to get her out of the line of fire. At the same time, he was able to stand with his leg right against the edge of the table.

Sidney covered him at once, his finger tight on the trigger and ready to fire. Ranz lifted his hands, palms out, to show that he was not trying anything.

'Easy, fella,' he said. 'I ain't got no reason to get killed over a woman. If you and this lady don't see eye to eye, it don't matter to me at all.'

Sidney grinned. 'You were quick enough to come to her defense earlier today. Why the change of heart?'

Ranz put on a casual mien. 'Hey, Sid, you know how that is. I was trying to act the part of a hero. I figured that she might be real grateful later.' He winked. 'You know what I mean?'

Sid widened his grin. 'Looks like it was working too. You two looked mighty cozy when I came in.'

'Women are all the same, Sid.' Ranz's voice was smug, laced with disdain. 'Be a little gallant for them and they'll fall into your arms. I didn't figure Cora here to be no different from any other female. Every one of them is a sucker for the right pitch.'

Cora spun to face him. 'Why you vile, sneaky, worthless convict!' She hissed the words with vehemence. 'I should've known that no man can be trusted. You're all a bunch of slimy snakes!'

Sid's eyes flickered toward Cora, amused at her reaction. It was all the edge that Ranz could hope to get. He knocked the table over with a push from his thigh, and then wrapped his arms around Cora and dragged her to the floor.

Sid fired his gun into the darkness, but he was in a panic. Three hasty shots and he retreated. Ranz had his own gun out, but the man was gone through the door. By the time Ranz reached the porch, there was no sign of Sidney.

Cora came up behind him, rubbing her elbow, while a number of people came running from all directions.

Ranz holstered his gun carefully. 'He got away, but he can't be far.'

Gus was the first to arrive. 'What happened?' he cried. 'We heard shots.'

'Sidney Bunk tried to get even for the beating I gave him,' Ranz replied. 'He ran off into the darkness.'

'He'll grab a horse and be gone before we can find him,' Jess spoke up. 'Want us to search for him?'

'No. Let him go. I don't think he'll come back – at least, not until the fighting is over.'

Gus held up his arms, motioning for the onlookers to be quiet. When all fell to silence, he took the floor.

'No fuss here, folks. It's that new fellow who rode in this afternoon. He's up to no good. Everybody keep a sharp eye. If you spot him, let me or Ranz know about it. We don't need a troublemaker in our midst.'

'He looked about as worthless as a thirteen of clubs,' one man said. 'Should've ridden him out on a rail this afternoon.'

'If I see him, he'll still get a splintery ride,' Jess chimed in.

The crowd broke up and went back to bed, and the two men who were on guard for the night returned to their posts. In a matter of a few minutes everything was as quiet as before the ruckus.

Ranz discovered that Cora had lit another

lamp in the room and was picking up the broken pieces of the one he had knocked over.

'That stepbrother of yours doesn't have a full stack of hay in his loft. You didn't tell me that about him.'

Cora kept her back to him while she worked. He wondered what was in her head. She was suddenly very cool and aloof.

'Something bothering you, Cora?'

'Nothing,' was her curt reply.

'Look, I don't blame you for the actions of Sidney. You didn't pick him for a stepbrother.'

'That isn't it.'

'So something is stuck in your craw,' he challenged. 'What is it?'

She kept her back to him and shook her head. As he approached, she moved quickly out of reach.

'For the love of sunshine, Cora, you're acting like one very strange creature.'

'Me?' she cried. *'Me?'*

Ranz knew that he had stepped into it right up to his lower lip. The problem was, he did not know what to do about it.

'Honestly, Cora, I don't know what I've done to make you mad at me.'

She kept her back toward him. 'I'm not

mad at you.'

'You sure as the devil act like it. If it isn't because of your brother, I–'

'Stepbrother,' she corrected him.

'Yeah, yeah, your stepbrother.'

'I told you, that isn't a problem. You saved us from being shot, and I'm beholden to you. You were very *gallant* a second time.'

The bell went off in his head. Suddenly, he was all too aware of what the problem was. It was what he had said to get Sidney to drop his guard.

'Listen to me, Cora,' he said softly. 'I didn't mean one word of what I told Sid. I said those things to buy us some time. You can't believe I'd be so low as to actually think that way.'

She kept her back turned toward him. 'I don't know what to believe.'

He let out a deep sigh. 'Holding you close was probably the most rewarding few moments in my life. It wouldn't have been special if I had stooped to trickery to get you into my arms.'

The words seemed to bounce off of her granite facade. He tried once more.

'I know that you distrust men, but you don't have to worry about me. I wouldn't do anything in the world to hurt or betray you.'

Cora would not even turn and look at him.

'I'm right sorry that you don't have any faith in me at all. It means that having you in my arms for those few precious moments really didn't mean a thing.'

With that, he left her standing alone and went up to his room. He didn't bother to light the lamp, for he desperately needed his couple of hours of rest. There was a battle ahead, one that he had little chance of winning, and it would do no good to pine about Cora. If he and the others lived through the fight, he might make another effort to win her trust. If they were killed, what would it all matter?

Chapter Nine

Sidney walked the horse a hundred yards from town. Then he mounted up and sat in the dark. He was brooding over his misfortune and lost opportunities.

There had to be a way to get something out of a situation like the one in the valley. He had been certain that Cora would cower at the mere sight of him, but she had grown strong with her independence. She had even stood up to him. Things had certainly changed with the passing of a couple of years.

She was no longer the frightened little waif that he could torment and harass to tears. When she took a stance, there was fire in her eyes and spirit in her voice. It had been too long since she felt his wrath.

'Thinks she can cheat me out of what is rightfully mine,' he said aloud. 'Well, think again, Bummer. You ain't rid of me yet, not by a long shot.'

But that posed another problem. What could he do against the convict? Ranz Tanner was a hardened killer. He had knuckles like iron and a jaw to match. Sidney had hit him with everything he had and not even knocked him down. Then he had had the drop on him and lost that edge too. Realistically, he had to admit that he was no match for the criminal. He would have to let someone else handle him.

Sidney smiled. Maybe that would take care of itself. Considering the impending attack and the feud between the ranch owner and the town of Adobe Wells, the raid on the town might destroy everything. If the people in town beat off the attack, the owner of the Cross M would be really riled up. That might open another door for Sidney.

For a few minutes he studied the lay of the town. He remembered seeing the inner defenses. When the time to escape had come, he knew where to get out through the barricade. It would be as simple to return the same way.

Five hundred dollars is what I came for, he reminded himself. *I'll get it from the boarding house and Bummer or I'll see the place burned to the ground. If the attack doesn't level everything in sight, maybe Duke will shell out the five hundred to finish the job right.*

As he smiled, he flinched from the pain from his swollen nose and eyes. Ranz had broken his face in their fight. He owed that man something special. He would bide his time for the rest of the night. If the town survived the coming attack, he would make an offer to Duke. That offer would include a way of killing the convict. Sidney wanted him to pay the full price, to die hard.

Hold Bummer in your arms, Ranz Tanner, he sneered silently. Kiss her and hug her all you can, 'cause the two of you don't have long to live. I'm giving you both notice. The end is closer than you think!

Sidney kicked his horse into motion. On his way into town, he had seen a good place to hole up for the fight. It was high enough in the nearby hills that no one was likely to spot him, and yet he could still see the floor of the valley. He would watch for the outcome of the battle, and then decide which move to make.

Ranz was back on the line before first light. He had not waited for breakfast. A man used to travel and warfare, he was not accustomed to eating more than once or twice a day. As his supper had been late, he was not hungry in the slightest.

'Wider and deeper,' he told the workmen. 'When it's finished, do the same as we did at the other end. Cover it with canvas from one end to the other. We don't want anyone from the Cross M seeing what we have planned.'

'It might work once, but what about the second charge?' Jess paused to lean on the handle of his shovel. 'Once we don't have surprise on our side, it could come to a gun battle.'

Ranz paused from his digging. 'First things first, Jess. If we stop the cattle charge, we'll set up for the second defense. If they come at us shooting, then it'll be a bloody battle to the end.'

'I don't know,' Flanders grunted between shovels of dirt. 'I'm afraid Duke won't quit. He'll keep at it until we're all buried in this trench.'

'One battle at a time,' Ranz replied. 'Sting him hard and send him running. If he comes again, we sting him again.'

'And if he decides to starve us out?'

'Too slow for a man who wants revenge,' Jess interjected. 'He'll want this place leveled to the ground. He won't quit until he has beaten us or we have killed him.'

'There are other things we could do,' Ranz told the men. 'But we first have to survive the initial frontal attack. If we drive them back, then we'll see about turning the tables and putting an end to the fighting.'

Flanders sighed. 'We should've tried to get someone out to the fort. The soldiers could be here in two days.'

'Two days might be a lifetime,' Jess answered.

'And we can't spare a single man,' Ranz also spoke up. 'One gun could make the difference between winning or losing this war.'

Flanders shook his head. 'I still can't believe the old man intends to kill all of us. Nothing he can do will bring back his son.'

'A man don't think when he's mourning a loss,' Jess said. 'You saw him ride in with his gunmen. 'Get out or die,' he tells us. 'Get out of my valley.' Well, it ain't his valley. He might've run cattle here for a year or two before we arrived, but that don't make him owner of the world.'

They continued to work until the morning sun rose high in the sky. A little before it was straight up, the dust cloud appeared on the horizon.

Jess pointed at it and turned to Ranz. 'Sure as you're standing here, Mouse Davis sold us out. They done exactly what you said they might do. They're coming from the opposite end of town. If we hadn't dug that second ditch, we'd be overrun first thing.'

Ranz estimated that it would be at least thirty minutes before the cattle reached the edge of town. 'Have them bring the barrels and pour it into the trench. Stand by for my signal.'

Jess hurried off to do as ordered. Gus and Flanders moved up to stand at his side. All three stared at the cloud in the distance.

'Big herd,' Gus said. 'Think your plan will work?'

'If is doesn't, we'll have hoofprints up our backs. Where's Old Henry?'

'He's ready for your signal. He's in the first house, right at the edge of town.'

'Better get the kids and old folks to the boardinghouse. Everyone else man his position.'

'You want all of the men up front?'

'Let's see if they attack from the same direction as the stampede. We might have to defend any one side of town.'

Flanders hurried off, but Gus remained at Ranz's side. When Ranz looked at Gus, the man stuck out his hand.

'If this works or not, Tanner, we're beholden to you. Any chance we have is due to your experience and planning. I'm glad you took a hand and threw your chips into our game.'

Ranz took his hand in a firm shake. 'I only hope it turns out for the best. I've been in a fight against cattle ranchers before, but this is the first time I ever tried to defend a town.'

'Thanks all the same. If it works, we'll owe everything left to you. If we go down fighting, we would have done that, anyhow. Duke is going to find out that we're not a bunch of cowards to be run off from our homes.'

'I'll see you after we turn back the charge, Mayor.'

'Yeah, I hope so.'

Ranz watched him scamper toward his position. Then he pulled his gun and checked the loads. He had already looked over the chamber twice, but it gave him something to do.

Done picked yourself a wild bull to ride this time, he thought. *You get gored by his horns, and you might not get back up.*

He quickly checked the location of the other men. Jess stood by the trench, ready for action. He couldn't see Old Henry, but he knew that the man was standing by. The riflemen were in position, all as fearfully anxious as he was himself.

The sound of steps approached, and he discovered Cora behind him. She had come at a run from the boardinghouse, but she slowed to a walk at his curious look.

'What are you doing out here?' he asked when she was within earshot. 'The cattle will be on us in a matter of minutes.'

Ignoring his remark, she continued toward him until she could stand at his side. Shielding her eyes with her hand, she stared out over the vast, open prairie.

'Can you turn them back?'

Ranz let out a long breath slowly. 'I don't know. Cattle are crazy-wild when they're running. I've known them to stampede right off a cliff and kill themselves. Brains or common sense ain't their best quality.'

'All the children and old folks are safe. I ... I didn't want to have anything happen before I...' But she couldn't finish the sentence.

Ranz realized that she was fighting an inner war with herself. She refused to look at him, but she also seemed determined to finish what she had started.

'We don't have much time,' he prompted her.

'I was...' She boldly raised her gaze to meet his eyes. 'I have to apologize, Ranz. I was wrong to think that you were the kind of man to do a woman dirt. I had to tell you that before we ran out of time.'

He offered her a smile. 'Truce?'

That caused her own lips to curve upward. 'Truce.'

'See you after the skirmish.'

She looked off toward the approaching cloud of dust. 'Is that what you call this – a skirmish?'

'Nothing between us and victory but twenty or thirty gunmen and a thousand head of cattle. Yep, this is going to be some skirmish.'

She placed a gentle hand on his arm. He discovered her eyes full of worry and concern. Something stirred deep inside him, and only the desperation of the moment kept him from trying to take her into his arms.

'Be careful, Ranz. I've grown quite fond of you.'

'The Yankees couldn't kill me, and the Mexican army didn't get the job done, either. A lot of men have taken their best shot and I'm still here.' He patted her hand. 'I'll be around when this is over. You can count on it.'

She spun away from him and hurried to return to her boardinghouse. Ranz watched her go, experiencing pangs of a hunger. It was not a craving that could be slaked by food or drink. He knew that the only way to quench the hunger was to hold that woman in his arms.

Got to live through this first, Ranz, old sport, he told himself. *Maybe you'd best get your mind back on the business at hand.*

The brown cloud in the distance was drawing closer. Then the dark specks of the cattle appeared on the horizon. It would not take long for the herd to reach the town. Once the stampede started, the action would be fast and furious.

Ranz paused to cast his eyes skyward. 'I ain't prayed much in my life, God, 'cause I ain't never learned how to do it proper,' he whispered softly. 'This much I know, You've surely watched over me in the past. I hope You'll throw Your weight to our side this time, 'cause it ain't just for myself.' He searched for more words, but there was nothing left to be said. 'Amen' seemed woefully inappropriate, so he ducked his head and added a single word:

'Thanks.'

Chapter Ten

The rumble was barely audible, but Ranz had heard the running of cattle before. The herd was coming at a rapid pace, and it wouldn't be long before the riders began to shout and fire guns. The running cattle would stampede.

Ranz took up position where he could watch the approach of the herd. He also kept watch in other directions, wary of a sneak attack. He was at a disadvantage because he had never met Duke MacDermit and had no idea how the man would think. It was hard to enter a fight and use only defense. If he knew the man, he could plan against him, possibly even initiate an attack of his own.

There was the sound of muffled shots and high-pitched yells. The earth began to tremble under the pounding hooves of what appeared to be nearly a thousand head of cattle.

'Here they come!' Gus shouted the obvious. 'We're ready for them!'

Ranz pulled his gun, wishing he had a rifle

instead. He could make some noise, but a pistol had a limited range and not much stopping power against a full-grown steer.

'Stand by with the torch!' he called to Jess. 'Be ready to signal Old Henry!'

The ground trembled under his feet, and amid the thundering herd he could hear guns being fired and men yelling.

A great wall of frenzied, panicked cattle came boiling toward the exposed end of the settlement. Ranz stood in the middle of the street, waiting to give signals. He knew that, from all outward appearances, the Cross M men would think they had outsmarted the town. The end of the street was open and bare of any defenses. It was an open invitation to the stampeding cattle.

Closer came the great, moving body. Bawling steers with hooves pounding and horns raking the air. The cattle would be driven by fear alone, eyes wide and terrified, caught up in a mass hysteria. The only weapon against them would be surprise and shock.

Dust rose into the sky to form a low-lying cloud. The noise was comparable to that of a powerful locomotive, a runaway train. When the lead steers were a scant hundred yards away, Ranz gave the signal.

Old Henry set off four charges of dynamite. Each blast was spaced across the exposed end of town. The concussion was nearly drowned out by the stampede, but the explosions sent dust and rocks flying high into the air.

At nearly the same moment, the canvas was jerked away from the trench and a torch was thrown into the pool of coal oil. A fiery wall rose fifty feet into the air, and spewed hot, yellow-orange flame and black smoke.

The frightened cattle were in total confusion. The lead steers were driven by those behind, but the dynamite and fire divided the herd. Instead of coming through town, the mad charge turned to the left and right sides and toward the neighboring hills.

From his position, Ranz watched two riders and their mounts go down in the maze of rushing cattle. He knew there would be very little left of those men.

The rest of the Cross M riders veered away from the direction of the split herd, saving themselves. The stampede was out of control. They had no way to turn the cattle back toward the town.

A cheer went up from the ranks of the people in town. The initial assault had been a complete failure for Duke and his men, and it would take many hours to gather the cattle and attempt another charge. If the cattle ran for long, they would not be in any condition to muster another stampede for at least a day.

Ranz holstered his gun and continued to watch the cattle disperse into the hills. The fire died down as the fuel was consumed. It still billowed a dark smoke and filled the air with an acrid stench, but it was dying out. He had fought off the first attack, but what would be Duke's next move?

'It worked perfectly!' Gus was shouting at his side. 'Those cattle didn't have any idea of where to go. It worked perfectly!'

'I saw at least two riders go down in the midst of the stampede,' Ranz said. 'That isn't going to set well with Duke MacDermit.'

'No fault of ours.'

'Was his boy being killed any fault of yours?'

Gus sobered. 'I see what you mean. Now he can blame two or three more deaths on us. It'll certainly make him that much more determined to drive us out of the valley.'

'You know the man. What's likely to be his next move?'

The mayor considered that question for a

time. 'He'll want to crush us, to get revenge for his failed stampede. I'd guess that he will send everything he has against us.'

'Some of his men must have friends in town. Any idea how many he has to send against us?'

'Possibly twenty of the thirty will do whatever he tells them. I know there are a few who won't have a hand in driving us out.'

'Still long odds for the firepower we have.'

Old Henry appeared from out of his hiding place. He looked as spry as a young rooster. His near-toothless grin was wide and his eyes were full of glee.

'See how we showed them? Did you boys get a look at my fireworks?'

'You did just fine,' Ranz told him. 'The explosions sure did the trick. Do you have anything left?'

'A few sticks that were too old to trust.' He squinted at Ranz. 'But I can put together a little surprise package for you.'

'What kind of surprise?'

'Nitroglycerin, that's what.'

Ranz arched his brows. 'You can whip up nitroglycerin?'

'I done it a couple of times when I was younger. Sweat the sticks of dynamite and catch the liquid. A little bottle of that tossed in the right direction would work better than a burning fuse. It goes off on contact.'

'You might blow us all to bits!' Gus cried. 'I've heard of men being killed trying that trick.'

'Got to know what you're doing, is all. I ought to know what I'm talking about.'

'If you want to risk it, see what you can do. Let me know how much explosive power you end up with,' Ranz said.

'Sure thing.' Old Henry laughed and hurried back out to the solitary house beyond the perimeter of the town's defenses.

'He'll probably blow himself to the next world,' Gus said, shaking his head. 'Bet he hasn't handled any explosives in twenty years.'

Ranz grinned. 'It ain't been that long, Mayor. That fellow, Nobel, didn't invent the stuff till after the war was over.'

Gus let out a prolonged sigh. 'It seems like a lifetime ago that the war ended. Guess I'm getting old and forgetful.'

'Back to the problem at hand,' Ranz said. 'What can we expect from MacDermit next? Do you think he'll try to run a stampede through the town a second time, or will he send gunmen to shoot it out with us?'

'I think we might end up shooting.'

'Then we'll put our defensive plan into action. Have the women armed and ready. If an attack comes, we'll need them to watch the opposite side of town.'

'If he draws all his men together for an attack, there should be a chance to send someone for help.'

'You said that would take two days. When the idea was mentioned before, you didn't seem to think there would be time to get help, remember?'

'I'm thinking now that we should have risked it, Tanner. What can we hope to win but a stalemate? We can't kill all of them, and they are going to have a time trying to kill all of us.'

'They'll probably strike hard and make the town pay a dear price for resisting. If they hurt us, it might be enough to force some of the people to pull out. Once our ranks are broken, we'll never defend a town of this size.'

'What would you do if you were in his shoes, Tanner?'

'I'd want to get even for my losses,' Ranz said tightly. 'I think Duke is going to hit us as hard as he can.'

Duke stormed about the camp. A group of

dusty and weary riders sat or lay about on the ground. They were waiting for Duke's orders, but anguish and defeat shone in their faces.

'We lost Clem and Maynard,' Keats spoke up. 'There wasn't much left to bury, boss.'

'Where did that bunch of dirty nesters come up with such a defense?' Duke growled. 'I didn't know there was any dynamite around here for a hundred miles!'

'They use it from time to time in removing trees or rocks from the fields. I don't know who handled it, but he must be good. Between the four explosions and that wall of fire, the cattle about took all of us out.'

Duke swore vehemently. 'Who's behind it? Do you think it's that convict?'

'Be my guess,' Keats replied. 'Like me and Con told you, the man looked capable.'

As Duke pointed at Con, the veins stuck out on his forehead from his fury. 'I want that man, Velarde! Give him to me – dead!'

'You've got it, boss,' Con replied. 'I'll figure out a way to get to him.'

Duke kicked a mound of dirt and sent up a cloud of dust. He swore savagely again. 'You might have killed Mouse too soon. He could have told us how to break their defense. If that killer is in charge, no telling what kind of protection he has around the town. We don't know how to go about an attack.'

'This is getting expensive, Mr. MacDermit,' Stringer spoke up hesitantly. 'We lost two men and about a hundred head of cattle on one single charge. There are a number of steers down from the heat. We could end up losing twice that many.'

Duke glared at him. 'You turning tail on me, Stringer? You want to cut and run?'

Stringer's face was a tight mask. 'You know me better than that, Mr. MacDermit. I ride for the brand.'

'Then what's your point?' Duke growled. 'Are you crying for us to quit before we even get started?'

'I'm making a point, that's all. I'm willing to drive those people out and burn their homes to dust, but I draw the line at killing any women or children, even if they're no better than carpetbaggers.'

Duke glowered at him. 'The stampede might have killed a dozen women and children. Didn't you think about that?'

'No. As a matter of fact, I didn't think about it. I really expected those people to have moved out and deserted the place. I don't rightly see nothing in Adobe Wells worth dying over.'

'That was my figuring as well,' Locker joined in. 'Who would have thought that a bunch of squatters would stand and make a fight of it?'

Duke glared at his men. He knew they weren't cowards. This first assault had been a total failure and it had hit them hard. He had to figure a way to give them a victory, even a small one.

'Are you with me or not?' he asked. 'I've declared war on Adobe Wells, and that means crushing all that oppose me. What do you men say?'

'I'll back you,' Con spoke up first. 'Those leeches stood by and let Stocker be killed in cold blood. I'm with you, boss.'

Keats stood up straight and faced Duke. 'You know we're behind you, whatever you decide. We won't let you down.'

Duke showed an instant relief at the vote of confidence. He swept over the men's faces and found what he wanted in their expressions.

'Let's find out if they have the stomach for a real fight,' he said. 'Soon as it gets dark, we'll slip down there in two teams and hit the town. Shoot anything that moves and set fire to any building you get close to. We'll make them think twice about sticking around my valley.'

'How far do we go?' Keats asked. 'Do we take the entire town?'

'If you can manage it, go ahead.' Duke paused, pointing a finger at him, then sweeping it over each man. 'But I don't want none of you getting killed. You drive hard at them and hammer them with bullets, but don't any of you get careless. If the defense is too strong, pull back and try a different side of town. They don't have enough people to guard all four sides at one time.' He waited for any comment, but no one offered to speak up. 'That's it, then. Get a couple of hours' rest and some grub.' His voice had turned to ice. His eyes were full of hate and his face was contorted with malice. 'Then we're going to run out a pack of coyotes!'

From high in the hills, Sidney Bunk watched the action. Begrudgingly, he gave credit to the people of Adobe Wells for turning the herd of cattle. If not for that trick, the buildings would have been ripped from the face of the earth.

He had an army field glass and he used it to survey the withdrawal of the cattlemen.

149

He could vaguely make out their camp, a mile or so away. They were mere specks in his field glass, but he could watch their moves.

Once certain that they were holed up for the afternoon, he concentrated on the town. He kept an eye on each of the four makeshift walls, noting any weakness in their defense.

Stupid cattlemen, he thought. *If they had half a brain among them, they'd have a man sitting up here. It ain't no problem seeing where to attack if you know how the town is setting up its defenses.*

That prompted him to think again about going to the Cross M with what he knew. If he had a little more to bargain with, he could get himself a nice stake out of this situation. Which was why he'd come to Arizona in the first place.

His heart turned to a fist of iron and his stomach churned. A seething rage nearly caused him to crush the field glass in his hands. The mere thought of Cora's winning out destroyed his common sense and self-control.

'No way, Bummer!' he snarled. 'You ain't getting off that easy!'

He wrestled with the wild impulse to ride

over to the cattleman at once. He needed more leverage. The information he could gather would be worth his price, but the ranch owner had to be desperate.

Sidney picked up his canteen and took a drink. The pressure of the metal against his lips caused him to flinch. His mouth was bruised and puffy. The split lip was twice its normal size, and even the tepid water hurt his loose teeth.

He silently vowed to put an end to Ranz Tanner. Whether it took a bullet in the back or an ambush during the night, he would get the job done. That man had beaten him twice, and Sidney Bunk did not take a loss lying down.

Recalling Cora in the man's arms, Sidney almost grew sick with his fury. Nothing had worked out for him. That girl had always been an open wound. She had come between him and his mother and then with Aunt Grace. She should not have been a part of his life at all, but there she was, always ruining everything.

He was only a child when she came to live with them. His own mother had turned from him to tend to the baby girl, and soon she no longer had any time at all for him. It was always Cora this and Cora that. Oh, his mother usually took his side once they were older, but obviously it was an effort to make up for her past neglect, and it did not work. He hated that child, that girl, and now that woman Cora Ankers.

He had not changed his own name from Bunk. His mother had never asked him why. She did not care why. Widowed twice in ten years, she had time only for working at the town bakery and tending that brat.

A cruel smile played along his swollen lips. Cora never knew the truth. She had never figured it out. He could not blame her for that, as only his mother's dying words had informed him of the unknown facts about Cora. He wondered how smug and important she would feel if he were to tell her what he knew.

'Maybe I'll let you in on a little secret, Bummer.' He slurred the words in his hate and bitterness. 'Think I'll figure a way to watch your convict pal get his due. Afterward, you and I can have a little chat. I wonder if you'll be so high and mighty once you know the truth.'

He put the glass to his eye and watched the town once more. He could see an old man cross to the only house on the end of town that was not within the defensive perimeter.

He didn't know the man's name, but he had seen him setting the dynamite charges.

'Looks like the doorway I've been looking for,' he mused. 'What do you say, old man?'

He let the plan take shape in his head. If the Cross M suffered another failure, they would be willing to deal with him. From the looks of the people fortifying the town, there was a good chance that they would beat back the cattlemen a second time.

'Hate to see you win a second battle, Adobe Wells, but I could use the victory. Beat them back once more and they'll be willing to pay my price.'

Chapter Eleven

The shroud of darkness covered the land and brought with it flashes from rifle muzzles and cracks of gunfire. Ranz led his group to meet the assault. They spread out and took cover among the barricade.

The attackers fired and moved fast, trying to close the distance between them and the nearest buildings. The glow of fire brightened the sky as the two outside houses at the far end of town were burned to the ground.

A second group hit the west end of town, but Gus was there with the other men to beat them back. When a few men tried to circle and enter the town from an exposed side, the women opened fire and sent them running.

Ranz moved from place to place, trying to figure out Duke's strategy. He was in position to see the women start shooting. In spite of the desperate situation, he had to smile. They really peppered the four cattlemen. Actually, a couple of them were much better shots than most of the men.

By the time he reached Gus, the cattlemen had broken off the attack. The two houses at the one end of town were still smoldering, but Old Henry had defended the lone shack at the opposite end. He refused to let the raiders get close to it even though it was beyond the barricade.

'Looks like we gave them what-for again,' Gus said. 'Maybe we won't have to get the Army to help us after all. We make a pretty good army all by ourselves.'

Ranz smiled. 'Soon as I check the rest of the posts and set up the night guards, I'll slip out and see how Old Henry fared.'

'He waved at us right after the shooting stopped. I think he's all right.'

'Tough old bird, that fellow. Won't give up that shack without a fight. Anyone would think that he owned it.'

'I imagine you know that he lives at the boardinghouse. Plain and simple, I think he enjoys being in this fight. It makes him important.'

'He sure proved his worth with the explosive charges today. Maybe folks have been shortchanging him.'

'I know that *I* have. Makes me durned sorry that I ever made fun of him. All of this

156

time I thought his stories were so much bunkum. From what I've seen these past few hours, I do believe I've misjudged him.'

'Anyone hit?' Ranz asked.

'One leg wound, but it's only a scratch. We never gave them a target to shoot at.'

'I'll see you later. Who has the next watch at this end?'

'Old Henry has it till midnight. Then he said that you were going to join him at the shanty and keep watch until daylight.'

'Yeah, I remember. I'll be back after I make the rounds.'

'When do you get to sleep?'

'Tomorrow, if nothing else happens. Be tough for the Cross M to sneak up on us in full daylight.'

'Okay, Tanner. I'm going to catch a few winks, as soon as I make sure everyone knows the schedule. See you later.'

Ranz left the mayor and went from place to place, checking on the damage. The people had all done their jobs well. None of the attackers had gotten close enough to penetrate the outer defenses. It was the second victory for Adobe Wells. Ranz didn't know how long their luck would hold, but MacDermit was bound to be getting flustered.

Ranz also wondered how the Cross M

men were feeling. Gus had said that some of them wouldn't fight against the town. It was difficult to tell how many men had been in the night assault, but it couldn't have been more than twenty. That gave him some hope. Maybe Duke would call off his war before the men turned on him or quit.

The house was quiet. Four men had been treated for various injuries, but they were all bunked down for the night. As a precaution, Duke had several night riders out to keep watch over the place and the cattle.

Smoking his pipe, Duke sagged deeply into his favorite leather-bound chair. Bitter defeat was mixed with the relentless sorrow he felt over the loss of his boy. The entire world had turned corrupt and now opposed him unjustly.

His mind wandered back to the beginning, back to that first group of settlers. They had arrived in four wagons without even a prayer, and Stocker had talked him into letting them settle the valley. His boy had taken a shine to one of the petticoats and that was the beginning of Adobe Wells.

Year after year the place grew. He'd watched them come in and spread out until they covered the valley floor. They used much of his summer water and tilled the bottomland for corn, beans, and squash. From three run-down shanties they had built a fair-sized town. There was even talk of building a school and using it on Sunday for a church. All that growth, and he had let it continue for his boy's sake.

Stocker had wanted a place to go and let loose. He had loved to play cards, drink, and brawl. Having a town nearby was better than letting him be gone for days on end, visiting the more distant towns and cities. At least, that had been Duke's thinking before Stocker's death. Everything looked different to him now. He didn't want the town on his land. Adobe Wells stood like a landmark to his son's murder. He wanted to wipe out all memory of Stocker's death. That would be complete only when the buildings were rubble and the people were driven out of the country.

The door opened, and he turned to see who had entered without knocking. He was not surprised to find Con Velarde standing in the next room. He never waited to be invited inside.

'In here,' Duke said.

Con showed his mirthless smile. 'I've a surprise for you, boss. Could be the very thing we need to turn the tide of this war.'

'And what's that?'

Con nodded to someone who was beyond Duke's view. An unfamiliar man entered the house. He removed his hat to reveal a face that was swollen and showed the dark bruises of a recent beating.

'This here is Sidney Bunk. He has some interesting information to sell us.'

Duke rose to his feet. He tapped his pipe against the edge of the fireplace and put a hard scrutiny on the new man.

'You say he wants to sell us something?'

'Claims he can get me inside Adobe Wells. He knows where the convict hangs his hat at night.'

That piqued Duke's interest. 'You don't say?'

Sidney straightened his shoulders importantly. 'I can give you a victory, Mr. MacDermit. I can get your man inside town. Once you dispose of that killer, you can ride like a king over the rest of Adobe Wells, because he's the brains behind their defenses.'

'He's something of a wonder man, beating us off twice,' Duke said. 'How does he do it?'

'I'd say the man knows a little about warfare. He knows how to deploy his forces and make the most of what he has to work with. On that sweep attack you tried tonight, your men encountered nothing but a handful of women at one side. They fired a volley of shots and then Tanner arrived with several men to back them up. If not for him, you'd have destroyed the town with the stampede. He's the one you need to be rid of.'

'And you're willing to help?'

Sidney showed a cocky smirk. 'Like I said, I can tell you how to get inside the town's defenses. I know how to get your boys right to Tanner.'

'And what's your price for this help?'

'I stand to lose five hundred dollars if the town is leveled. That's my asking price.'

Duke looked at Con. 'What do you think?'

'Sounds like a chance we ought to take, boss. If I could take out Tanner, the people would break and run. He's the key to winning this battle.'

The Cross M owner rubbed his chin thoughtfully. 'One condition, Bunk. You take Con in yourself. I don't intend to have him walk into an ambush.'

That was to Sid's liking, and he nodded at once. 'Sure, I'll do that. I can take him right to that convict's bed.'

'You fulfill your end of the bargain and I'll

161

give you the five hundred dollars. That fair enough?'

'Yes, sir. I'm sure that you're a man of your word.'

Duke turned his attention to Con. 'Think the town figures us to do anything more tonight?'

Con showed his usual twisted grin. 'I think we might catch them all sleeping. Ought to be near midnight when we get to town. Won't be more than a couple of guards to avoid.'

'That's right, Mr. MacDermit,' Sidney said. 'Tonight would be the ideal time to strike. After beating you back, they won't be expecting anything more.'

'All right, Con. You try it your way. Want any more men to ride with you?'

'More men, more chance of being seen,' Con replied. 'Me and Sidney will tend to this chore alone.'

'Good luck. I'll be waiting up to hear from you.'

Ranz paused at the smokehouse and listened to the sounds of the night. It was uncomfortably quiet. Not a cricket chirped, not a whisper of air moved. Why did it bother him that the raid had been a bust and Duke had called off his dogs for the night?

Back in the heart of town, only the night guards were out and about. Everyone else had turned in for a few hours of sleep. Things were peaceful and serene. He should have been glad to have it that way.

Even in the dead of night, Ranz walked along in the shadows. It wouldn't pay to parade down the middle of the street and discover that the Cross M had a sniper close by.

Ranz reached the outer limit of the town barricade and slipped through a small opening. Then he quickly darted across to the small shack. It was time to relieve Old Henry.

'I'm coming in, Henry,' he whispered. 'Don't get trigger-happy.'

There was no reply, so Ranz pushed through the back door. He couldn't see in the darkness of the room. The lone window had a blanket over it.

'You in here, Henry?'

Hearing a barely audible moan, Ranz groped for the lamp and put a match to it. As he turned up the light, he saw Old Henry lying on the floor.

Ranz dropped next to the man and examined him quickly. A deep puncture wound was between his ribs, and his breathing was ragged and uneven. He'd been stabbed and was about gone.

'What happened, Henry?' he asked, lifting the man's head gently. 'Who did this?'

Old Henry set the rotted stumps of his teeth together, fighting the waves of pain. His eyes opened to mere slits.

'Watch ... watch yourself,' he gasped. 'Con Velarde is ... is in town.' His eyes rolled back and he closed the lids tightly. 'Caught me napping, Tanner.'

'Rest easy, Henry. I'll get someone to–'

Old Henry's hand found Ranz's wrist. He gripped tightly. 'No ... no time, son.' He coughed and doubled up for a moment, then fought to regain control. With a super-human effort, he pointed toward the table.

'There you are, there ... in the bottle.'

Ranz checked the room and spotted a small flask of clear liquid. 'That the nitro?'

Old Henry could only nod.

Ranz felt that he had let Old Henry down. 'If only I'd have come sooner. I could have–'

But the old man shook his head. 'Heck, son, I didn't want to ... to get so stove up that I couldn't get around. This is better for me.'

'You're a real hero, Old Henry,' Ranz told him. 'I mean that. We could never have turned those cattle without you.' He swallowed the lump that threatened to take away his voice. 'And that bottle of nitro might put an end to this feud altogether.'

A smile spread across the old man's face. 'You mean it? I'm a sure-enough hero?'

'No one in town will ever forget you. We're going to win the war against the Cross M and it'll be because of you.'

Old Henry delighted in the praise. He squeezed Ranz's arm a second time, and the thread of a smile played on his lips. Then his facial muscles grew limp, his mouth fell open, and a deep sigh escaped his lungs. The man was dead.

Cora had been waiting up for Ranz. She knew that he had not taken time to eat, and it was her intention to feed him and perhaps talk with him for a while. If he was not too tired, she had many questions that needed answers.

When the door opened, she ran to greet him. But her heart sank as quickly as it had leaped, for there stood her stepbrother.

'Hello again, Bummer.' His eyes flicked about the room as if searching for someone.

'You alone?'

Cora took a step back. 'The women and children returned to their homes, but several of the men are sleeping upstairs.'

Sidney laughed. 'You never could lie worth a hoot. You're alone, and you're up and waiting for someone.' A dark fire danced in his eyes. 'Wouldn't be that killer man, would it?'

Cora looked for a weapon. She was desperate to drive Sidney out of her place and out of her life. That thought was quickly dashed, for Con Velarde entered behind him.

'You said he'd be here!' Con growled. 'If this is a double cross, I'll make sure you don't live to enjoy it!'

Sidney shook his head quickly. 'He'll be here. He must be out making the rounds. His room is right upstairs. All we have to do is wait for him.'

'You miserable snake!' Cora snapped. 'You sold us out!'

'My, my, Bummer. Is that any way to talk to your loving stepbrother?'

She bore into him with burning, hateful eyes. 'There never was any love between us. You saw to that.'

He curled his lips into a sneer. 'And you were always innocent and sweet, I suppose?'

'I was much younger than you. I had no

way to fight back.'

'You've always been a pain to me, Bummer. From the day you arrived in my house, I've hated everything about you.'

'I didn't deserve that hate. I never did anything to you.'

He grunted in contempt. 'Sure, you never did anything, except come between me and my mother, and Aunt Grace took you under her wing and kicked me out of her life. All you ever did was encourage it a little.'

'Your mother always took your side in our fights. As for Grace, she was a kind and gentle woman, someone you had nothing in common with!'

Con had closed the door and moved to the dark shadows in the room. He kept watch out the window but was careful not to show himself. It appeared that he had a deaf ear turned toward both of them.

Cora's mind was working while she engaged in a verbal confrontation with Sidney. If she kept him preoccupied, she might have a chance to warn Ranz.

A cruel smirk shone on Sidney's battered face. 'I learned something about dear Aunt Grace a few months back.' His voice grew cold and brittle. 'It was on Mother's deathbed.'

Cora sucked in her breath. 'Mother? She ... she's...'

'She died last winter. That's when I decided to come pay you a visit.'

'Grace didn't tell me.'

'Mother come down sick and didn't have time to write. I told her that I would get in touch with you. I got your letter about Grace a week or so before Mother died.'

'I'm sorry,' she said, saddened by the loss.

'I really did love your mother. She was the only mother I ever knew.'

'That's not exactly true, Bummer.'

Her grief was instantly replaced by suspicion. 'What do you mean?'

Sidney had a self-satisfied look on his face. 'All these years you've been casting that pious shadow, prancing about with your nose in the air. I've grown sick to death of watching you. Little Miss Goody-Goody, the sweet and innocent girl.'

'Since when is it a sin to be nice to other people?'

'You think you're an innocent victim, picked on by a cruel, unfeeling stepbrother.' There was a sadistic smirk on his puffy lips. 'Well, it's time you learned the truth.'

'What truth is that?' she asked while continuing to keep watch for Ranz. A scream would warn him, even if it endangered her own life.

'Ever wonder why your father never told you about your mother?'

'Father didn't like to talk about it.'

A dark light glowed again in Sidney's eyes. 'Ever wonder why he and Mother never went to see Aunt Grace, not even once before he died?'

'Mother wouldn't tell me, and Grace would never talk about it. I always supposed that Mother didn't get along with her, and Father sided with his wife.'

Sidney laughed at that. 'Just the opposite, Bummer. Exactly the opposite.'

It was Cora's turn to frown in suspicion. 'What do you mean?'

'Aunt Grace was *my* Aunt Grace, my mother's sister.'

'So?'

He appeared extremely pleased with himself when he next spoke. 'So she was not your Aunt Grace. You two were much closer than that.'

'What are you saying?' Cora's voice was only a whisper as her heart ground to a halt.

'Aunt Grace was your mother, Bummer. That's why she favored you so much over me. That's why she wanted you to have her money. That's why my mother never spoke to her and Father never went to visit her. You are illegitimate, Bummer, born out of wedlock!'

She was stunned. Her brain flooded by an ocean of emotions, she could not think but could only feel. A terrible mixture of sensations washed over her, from the elation of knowing that Grace was her real mother to the shame of realizing that she was illegitimate.

Sidney scoffed at her pained expression. 'Poor Aunt Grace,' he taunted her. 'The poor woman had been done dirt by some man.' His laugh was cruel. 'Poor old tramp! That's what she was – a tramp!'

'No!' Cora cried. 'It isn't true! It can't be true!'

Her stepbrother displayed an obvious disgust. 'Try to get it straight in your head, Bummer. You have to face facts. You were born out of wedlock. That makes you a–'

Cora slapped him so hard that her hand stung from the force of the blow. It was the only lick she got in.

Sidney recovered instantly and struck back. His palm was not open for a slap, however. When his fist made contact with Cora's jaw, it was doubled and as hard as granite.

She staggered back from the punch and hit the table. Dazed from such a blow, she found herself sitting on the floor. Sidney stood over her, his fists at his sides.

'Get up and I'll smash in your face!'

'Shut up, Bunk!' Con ordered. 'Do you want to bring every gun in town down on us?'

At almost the same time, there was the sound of running feet out on the porch. Con backed away from the window.

'Put out that lamp!' he told Sidney.

'What is it?' Sidney cried. 'What's going on?'

Con's face was dark with rage. His gun was out and pointed right at him. 'You stupid moron! The place is crawling with gunmen. They've surrounded us.'

'Give it up!' Gus called from out in the dark. 'You've no way out, Velarde. We've got the place totally covered. Don't make us kill you.'

The blood drained from Sidney's face. He stared into the muzzle of the gun and took a step backward.

'Wait a minute, Con. I didn't give nothing away. I don't know how they discovered us. Maybe Old Henry lived long enough to talk.'

'You killed Old Henry?' Cora murmured. 'Poor Old Henry.'

Con looked around the room quickly and made a decision. 'There might be a chance to escape, but it'll mean taking the girl hostage.' His cruel smile lifted his lips. 'There are only two horses waiting for us.'

'Hold on, Con. I can see what you're thinking, but–'

A blast from Con's gun put a sudden end to Sidney's sentence. Sidney grunted and looked at his chest. He touched the small hole in his shirt and drew back a smear of blood.

'I ... I'm on your ... your ... side...' His words trailed off and he collapsed on the floor in a heap.

'You can live or die, woman!' Con's face was flushed with excitement. 'Get over here – right now!'

Chapter Twelve

Ranz held his breath. He exchanged looks with Gus. 'Anyone hit?'

'The shot wasn't fired at us,' Gus replied. 'You don't think that he shot–'

'Out there in the street!' Con shouted from inside the building.

'We hear you,' Gus called back.

'I've got the woman with me. You try anything, and she gets a bullet in the brain. You listening to me?'

'You can't get away, Velarde. Don't make it any worse for yourself.'

Con uttered a spiteful laugh. 'What worse? You can only hang a man once. I know that you must have found Old Henry's body. That's what tipped you off.'

'What's the deal, Velarde?' Gus asked. 'There's no need to hurt that woman.'

Con called back, 'I'm leaving this here place and she's going with me. If you try anything, I'll kill her. That ought to be simple enough for you to understand.'

Gus looked at Ranz. 'What do we do?' he

asked quietly. 'We can't risk getting Cora killed.'

'Let him go. I'll get my horse and try and take him on the trail. If I miss, I'll follow right to the Cross M ranch.'

'You can't handle that alone. There are a dozen gunmen at the ranch.'

But Ranz didn't argue the point. 'You just let him go. I'll be in touch with you.'

Ranz hurried off into the dark. He had picked up the bottle of nitro that Old Henry had prepared. It was safely stored next to his gear. When he saddled his horse, he took the bottle and tucked it into his shirt.

Once ready, he headed toward the main trail to the Cross M. He had already decided against trying to ambush Con in the dark. One slight mistake and Cora might be injured or killed. Besides that, he had to move very carefully with the bottle of explosive. One bump would mean the end of him and his horse.

Moving through the dark, he had only a vague idea of where the ranch was located. It would be to his advantage to reach the place before Con Velarde and Cora. If he could take them by surprise, before they were ready for a counterattack, he might get her out of there safely.

His horse was surefooted. He hit a main trail about a mile out of town and decided it was probably the one he needed to take. He kept a sharp eye both ahead and behind. There might be a night guard in front of him, and Velarde would be coming up from the rear. He needed to sneak into the ranch unseen.

An hour up the trail he glimpsed some distant specks of light. He veered off the main road and cut through a stand of trees. With his horse picking his way carefully, he circled far to the side of the ranch. Then he rode to within five hundred yards of the first building and stopped.

'This is as far as I dare take you,' he whispered to the horse. 'You stay here and be quiet. I don't want you howdying any of the other nags, you hear me?'

The horse was already busy snatching up a mouthful of bunch grass. Ranz ground-reined the animal and slipped quietly forward.

The bunkhouse was dark, but the main building showed lights in two of its four rooms. It was a good-sized home. The walls appeared to be of thick timber and mortar, and the roof was covered with sod with a few weeds growing. Outer walls had been built to fortify the place against Indian attacks. The partitions stood four feet tall and circled the entire house. There was a front gate, but it was closed.

Ranz kept low and rushed up to the wall. He listened to the sounds of the night, but only a lonely cricket was chirping. If any of the men were around, they were being quiet or had fallen asleep.

After placing the bottle on the wall, Ranz hefted himself up and over it quietly. He stuck the flask back into his shirt and tiptoed up to the side of the house. Ever so carefully, he risked a peek into the nearest window.

The room was empty. A solitary lamp was burning on the table, but there was no one visible. He decided that he had beaten Yelarde to the ranch. That was a big step in his favor.

An idea struck him, and he tried the window. It groaned slightly, then gave way to his prying fingers. It opened outward, and he stuck a leg through and ducked into the room. With any luck, they wouldn't know he was on the grounds, let alone inside the main house. That would double his edge and give him a chance to rescue Cora.

Quickly pulling the window closed, Ranz

went over to a shelf on the wall. It had a number of bottles and glasses, and it was Duke's own bar for entertaining his guests. He removed the nitro and set the flask up next to the other bottles. Then he moved quietly over to peer into the next room. It was the kitchen.

The sound of horses alerted him. He ducked out of the lighted room and listened from inside the kitchen.

'What in thunderation are you doing with that female?' Duke's voice came from the front of the house.

'That slicker led me into a trap. I had to take the gal hostage to get out of town.'

'What a fine human being you are!' Cora cried. 'You attack a town with your gunmen and then stoop to murder and kidnapping.'

'Shut up, woman!' Duke roared. 'You're the one who got my boy killed. You're the Ankers gal!'

'Don't blame me for your not ever teaching your offspring manners, Mr. MacDermit. He attacked me right in the middle of the street.'

There was an odd sound, as if someone had been pushed or hit. Something hit the ground and grunted from the impact.

'Ought to do more than knock her off her high horse!' Duke was still enraged. 'Ought to string her up from the highest tree on the place!'

Con chuckled. 'She ain't as high and mighty as you might think, boss. She came into this world out of wedlock. She's a base-born brat, that's all she is.'

Duke also laughed. 'You don't say? Cora Ankers is illegitimate!'

'That slicker was her stepbrother. I had to listen to the two of them squabble and fight for a full ten minutes. I'll tell you, boss, I'd sooner have shot it out with the whole town.'

There was a pause, and then Duke said, 'Bring her inside. We'd better sort this out. The people in town won't stand for our taking a hostage.'

'It was the only way to get out with my life. They had me surrounded.'

'Don't worry about it, Con. We'll put an end to Adobe Wells tomorrow. I've got a plan that can't fail.'

They were talking as they walked into the house. Ranz pulled his gun and waited for his chance. If they locked Cora away, he might grab her and escape. If they decided to get rough, he'd kill them both right off. He wouldn't stand by and let Cora be hurt.

'You say you have a plan?' Con was asking.

'I seen the Indians do it once. They set fire to several wagons full of hay and straw and ran them into the barricades and outlying houses. We'll burn the place down around their ears.'

Ranz set himself and waited. Once he knew what they intended to do with Cora, he would make his move. It would be a death-defying ride, trying to escape the ranch, but he had no other choice.

Something hard and cold pressed into his back. He froze in position. A voice growled:

'Don't even twitch, fellow, or I'll send you to your Maker with a big hole in your back!'

Chapter Thirteen

'Ranz!' Cora cried, seeing him herded into the room. 'You shouldn't have come!'

'Found his horse back from the house a ways,' the man behind him explained. 'Took me a few minutes to spot him in the kitchen, but here he is.'

Duke beamed. 'Good work, Locker. You done just fine.'

Con pulled his own gun while the man called Locker took Ranz's gun. Ranz was then shoved over to stand next to Cora. When he saw the swelling on the side of her face, he glared at Velarde.

'You're pretty tough with a woman. Give me half a chance, and I'll see if you've got any guts against a man.'

Con blinked in surprise and then smiled again. 'Not me, tough guy. I don't knock women around. It damages the hands.' He narrowed his gaze. 'I need these hands for handling a gun.'

'He didn't hurt me,' Cora said quickly. 'Sidney hit me before Con killed him in cold blood.'

Ranz simmered. 'Sounds like you did me a favor, Velarde. Maybe I owe you two debts. You let me out of the prison wagon and now you stick up for my girl.'

'Don't make too much of the second. I killed that skunk for getting me into a mess. I figured that no one would miss him. As for letting you out of the wagon, that proved to be a big mistake.'

'There's no need to go on with this fighting.' Ranz turned his attention to Duke. 'Your boy was killed by Joe Brady, and Joe Brady is dead. What sense does it make to run everyone out of the valley?'

'Ain't no room for discussion on that subject,' Duke said. 'Everyone is going to clear out of my valley or end up buried in it. That ought to be simple enough for anyone to understand, even you.'

'Then you intend to kill those who oppose you?'

Duke puffed up his chest. 'I think I've proved that much, bucko. And now that I've got you, the rest will be easy.'

'What are you going to do with the lady here?'

He spat in disgust. 'Lady? I don't see no lady. She got my boy killed and she's misbegotten to boot. I think you and she will share the same fate – hanging at the end of a rope.'

Ranz was in line with the window he had pushed open. It was closed now, but it was not locked or shut tight. If he could catch them off guard somehow...

'I'm sorry, Ranz.' Cora leaned closer to him. 'This is all my fault.'

Then Ranz surprised everyone in the room, including Cora. He took her in his arms and kissed her.

Duke was dumbfounded. 'What the devil is...?'

'A last kiss,' Con said with a laugh. 'One last kiss before they die.'

'Ain't it touching?' Locker was also laughing at the exhibition.

Ranz was glad that Cora responded. Whether it was out of her own fear or just a desperate last act, he didn't know. Either way, he was able to lean her around in line with the window.

Without warning Cora, Ranz went into motion. He already had her in his arms, so he jerked her off of her feet and went into a dive at the window. His head and shoulders knocked it open and the two of them fell out onto the ground.

'Run!' he shouted, giving her a push toward the darkness.

Con, Locker, and Duke ran over to the window. Even as their faces appeared, Ranz threw a handful of dirt and rocks at them. They pulled back. It gave him time to search out a few decent-sized rocks.

'Look out!' Con was laughing at the exercise in futility. 'He's throwing rocks at us.'

'Yeah, don't let him hit you!' Locker joined in.

'Stupid fool!' Duke growled. 'He can't possibly escape us in the dark without even a horse.'

Ranz threw the first rock and hit the far wall. He tried again and nailed a bottle of brandy.

'What an arm!' Con shouted, still not showing himself in the window. 'Bet he could daze a full-grown rabbit with one of those rocks.'

'Look out, everyone!' Locker was also enjoying the humor of the situation. 'He's throwing bigger rocks. Let's let him go. I don't want to face a man with a handful of rocks.'

'Summon the men and get after him!' Duke barked. 'I want him and the woman dangling from a tree by sunup.'

Ranz threw again, and then the world exploded in his face.

A blast of air, glass, and flame knocked him off his feet. He rolled over and over to get away from the debris as the house splintered and scattered in all directions at once. Hunks of wood and furniture came crashing down around him. And he heard the sizzle of cracked and burning wood.

'Don't move!' A frosty voice warned.

Ranz did move. He sat up slowly and ran his fingers over his face. Several splinters and a piece of glass were imbedded in one cheek.

'You're the convict, the one we let loose from the prison wagon.'

Ranz looked up to see Keats. Keats had his gun pointed right at his head.

'War's over, Keats. You don't have a boss or gunman running the place any longer.'

Keats looked toward the house. 'They were inside?'

'Con, Duke, and a man they called Locker. I didn't have a choice, Keats. They were going to kill both me and Cora Ankers.'

Several men came running into view. There was nothing left of the house. The roof and walls were gone. Even the bodies had been blown to bits.

'What's the deal, Keats?' a man asked.

'It's over, Stringer. The fighting is over.'

Ranz let out the breath he'd been holding, for Keats had holstered his gun. Keats told the other men:

'Locker was inside with Con and the boss. That was some explosion. I doubt we'll find enough of them to bury.'

'Nitroglycerin,' Ranz explained. 'They left me no choice.'

Cora came from out of the dark. She didn't speak, but knelt down to tend to Ranz. He flinched as she began to remove one of the splinters.

'You're welcome to stay the night,' Keats said. 'One of the boys can ride into town and tell them the war is over.'

'What will you do now, Keats?'

'Duke has a brother. I'll get in touch with him and see what he has to say. I would imagine he'll let me run the place for a share of the profit. There will be some changes made.'

Ranz managed to rise to his feet. He was unsteady, but no bones had been broken by the blast. A few inches closer, and he might have lost his head.

'If you've a mind to, I'd like to shake your hand, Keats. I think you're a man who knows what's right and what isn't.'

Keats took the hand and nodded gravely. 'Thanks to you, the killing has stopped. There's a difference between knowing what's right and *doing* what's right. From here on, I intend to be the *doing* kind.'

Gus and most of the town were there the next day to see Ranz off. The prison wagon was fixed and ready to roll. Ranz said his farewells to the others, but saved Cora for the last.

They led the team to the end of the street, walking side by side. When they stopped, it was next to the house where Old Henry had been killed.

'We won't forget him,' Cora said, her voice as soft as a brush of satin against bare skin. 'He died a hero. He saved our town.'

'He died with a smile on his face,' Ranz told her. 'He had no regrets. Can't ask for more than that.'

Cora lowered her head demurely. 'What about us, Ranz? I mean, I'll wait for you, if ... if you wish to ... to come back.'

'Might be gone for some time. Gus never got around to writing that letter for me.'

That put a spark in her eyes. 'Well, he certainly *will* write it. He'll write it today!'

He looked back toward town and pulled her over until the wagon hid them from view.

'As for you, I haven't quite decided about you yet, Cora. The only time I got to kiss you was at the Cross M. How do I know that you love me?'

She came into his arms and planted a warm, resounding kiss on his lips. The fire rose in his blood until he had to release her.

'You don't have to worry about me,' he told her. 'I'll be back before you know it.'

She grew serious. 'I'm not ... not legitimate. Don't you find that shameful?'

'We'll make sure that all our kids are legitimate. That ought to make amends for something that you had no control over.'

An ardent smile slowly lit her face. 'I love you, Ranz. If Gus can't get you a pardon, I'll write to you every day.'

'Five years is a long time.'

'I'll manage.'

He grinned. 'Then I'll try to cut the time a little shorter, to, say, about six days.'

Perplexed, she stared at him. 'Six days?'

'Guess it slipped my mind. Gus didn't write his letter because there was no need. The judge that sentenced me wrote a letter to Yuma on my behalf. The only reason I have to show up is to turn in this wagon and clear myself. I should be back within a week.'

'You – you sneak!' she cried. 'I've been worried sick, and all the time you were–'

Ranz knew how to handle such an outburst. He pulled Cora into his arms and kissed her. When he let go, she looked dreamily into his eyes.

'Sure you can't make it in less than six days?'

'I'm going to give it one heck of a try, Cora. Yes, ma'am, I'm going to give it a heck of a try!'

The publishers hope that this book has given you enjoyable reading. Large Print Books are especially designed to be as easy to see and hold as possible. If you wish a complete list of our books please ask at your local library or write directly to:

The Golden West Large Print Books
Magna House, Long Preston,
Skipton, North Yorkshire.
BD23 4ND